It was done. They were married— Sophie was his wife.

Thomas's stomach clenched at the word. How far had he come, from a Coast Guard chopper pilot content with his bachelor life to a man with a wife and ready-made family?

And how did Sophie feel about all of this? He couldn't read her at all. She veiled her emotions behind a bright smile.

She looked radiant, lovely. Demure, in an un-Sophie-like way, like a spear of sunlight cutting through the water on a gray day.

For one crazy second, he wished this was a regular wedding, that they were two people in love preparing to begin their lives' journey together. The fierceness of his desire startled him.

"She's a beautiful bride," someone murmured. "You're a lucky man, Thomas."

Lucky? He thought about the word. It shouldn't have fit, given the circumstances, but somehow it did.

He *was* lucky.

Dear Reader,

This is definitely a month to celebrate, because Kathleen Korbel is back! This award-winning, bestselling author continues the saga of the Kendall family with *Some Men's Dreams,* a journey of the heart that will have you smiling through tears as you join Gen Kendall in meeting Dr. Jack O'Neill and his very special daughter, Elizabeth. Run—don't walk—to the store to get your copy of this genuine keeper.

Don't miss out on the rest of our books this month, either. Kylie Brant continues THE TREMAINE TRADITION with *Truth or Lies,* a dicey tale of love on both sides of the law. Then pick up RaeAnne Thayne's *Freefall* for a haunting, mysterious, page-turner of a romance. Round out the month with new books by favorites Beverly Bird, who's *Risking It All,* and Frances Housden, who'll introduce you to a *Heartbreak Hero,* and brand-new author Madalyn Reese, who gives you *No Place To Hide* from her talented debut.

And, as always, come back again next month, when Silhouette Intimate Moments offers you six more of the best and most exciting romances around.

Enjoy!

Leslie J. Wainger
Executive Editor

Please address questions and book requests to:
Silhouette Reader Service
U.S.: 3010 Walden Ave., P.O. Box 1325, Buffalo, NY 14269
Canadian: P.O. Box 609, Fort Erie, Ont. L2A 5X3

Freefall
RAEANNE THAYNE

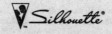

INTIMATE MOMENTS™
Published by Silhouette Books
America's Publisher of Contemporary Romance

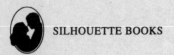

SILHOUETTE BOOKS

ISBN 0-373-27309-6

FREEFALL

Copyright © 2003 by RaeAnne Thayne

This edition published by arrangement with Harlequin Books S.A.

® and TM are trademarks of Harlequin Books S.A., used under license.
Trademarks indicated with ® are registered in the United States Patent
and Trademark Office, the Canadian Trade Marks Office and in other
countries.

Visit Silhouette at www.eHarlequin.com

Printed in U.S.A.

Books by RaeAnne Thayne

Silhouette Intimate Moments

The Wrangler and the Runaway Mom #960
Saving Grace #995
Renegade Father #1062
*The Valentine Two-Step #1133
*Taming Jesse James #1139
*Cassidy Harte and the Comeback Kid #1144
The Quiet Storm #1218
Freefall #1239

* Outlaw Hartes

RAEANNE THAYNE

lives in a graceful old Victorian nestled in the rugged mountains of northern Utah, along with her husband and two young children. Her books have won numerous honors, including several Readers' Choice Awards from *Romantic Times* and a RITA® Award nomination by the Romances Writers of America. RaeAnne loves to hear from readers. She can be reached through her Web site at www.raeannethayne.com or at P.O. Box 6682, North Logan, UT 84341.

Chapter 1

As final resting places go, the El Carmelito cemetery in Pacific Grove, California, was a beautiful place to spend eternity.

The wild sea off Point Piños crashed just a few hundred yards away, wind-gnarled Monterey cypress provided shade and serenity and a small herd of blacktail deer browsed among the grave markers.

Under other circumstances, Sophie Beaumont might have found some small comfort that her sister would be laid to rest here in exactly the kind of place Shelly had loved best. But she couldn't find anything remotely resembling comfort. Not yet. Not when the shock and grief of losing her twin so abruptly raged through her like that fierce ocean battering the rocks.

She hated funerals, she always had, and this one was by far the worst. Sophie swallowed hard as she looked at those elegant matching coffins waiting to be lowered into the ground—one starkly, horribly empty, one containing Shelly's battered remains.

She thought of the burial ritual she had seen a few months earlier in rural China, where mourners wore colorful clothing and celebrated the deceased's life with an exuberant funeral parade. Or the Jamaican way, where the families of the deceased dressed in their Sunday best and feasted for nine days. Shelly would have vastly preferred that to this cold, solemn ceremony.

Two small, sniffly whimpers on either side of her dragged her from her thoughts. Poor lambs. Poor bewildered little orphaned lambs. Her sister's own twins, Zach and Zoe, just five years old, didn't know what to make of this somber service. All they knew was their mother and father were both gone and that their comfortable, secure world had changed forever.

"Shh," their older sister, Alison, whispered to the twins. Her green eyes, far wiser than their ten years, looked at Sophie solemnly as if waiting for her to do something. Sophie gazed back helplessly, not sure what her niece expected of her. Finally, with a heavy sigh, Ali pulled her younger brother into her lap to console him.

Sophie winced. If she wasn't so tired, she would have thought of that. Or at least she wanted to think so.

Following Ali's example, she pulled Zoe into her own lap. The little girl snuggled against her with a few more sniffles, her cheek pressed against the black leather of the slim little blazer Sophie had picked up a few months ago at a market in Belarus. It was far too hot for leather, unexpectedly warm for a cloudy November day on the peninsula, but Sophie had had nothing else with her suitable for a funeral—and no time to find anything else— when Thomas had finally tracked her down two days earlier in Morocco. She'd been traveling nonstop since his call and barely made it to Monterey a few hours earlier, in time to shower and change out of her traveling clothes.

The preacher was droning on about walking through the valley of the shadow of death, about ashes to ashes, dust to dust. She wanted to listen but the words seemed hazy, surreal.

This couldn't be Shelly he was talking about in that dry, lifeless tone. Her sister had been funny and big-hearted, passionate about her children and deeply in love with her husband.

Whether the son of a bitch deserved it or not.

Loud, dramatic sobbing down the row of chairs cut through the minister's words like a chainsaw, and Zoe sniffled louder in her arms. Though she felt small and mean for it, Sophie wanted to stalk down the row of mourners and give her mother a good, hard slap. Couldn't Sharon tell she was upsetting the children with her wailing and carrying on?

Of course she couldn't, she answered her own question. And even if Sharon knew, she probably wouldn't care.

The minister droned on until Sophie wanted to scream at him to stop, that he obviously didn't know anything about Shelly if he thought his words carried any meaning about her life.

Zach sniffled again on Ali's lap and Sophie felt heat brush her shoulder. Not a touch, just a stirring of air. Automatically, her gaze shifted to the man sitting on the other side of her niece. Thomas Canfield, brother to Shelly's husband Peter, had wrapped an arm around Ali and pulled her close, Zach and all.

He looked solid and reassuring, his shoulders impossibly broad in his Coast Guard dress blues, and for one insane moment she wanted nothing more than to burrow her head against his chest as if she were five years old just like the twins.

Over the childrens' heads, their gazes met. Not a trace of warmth showed in those icy blue eyes. They were diamond-hard and so bitterly cold she shivered, despite her leather jacket and the heat of the afternoon.

She forced her attention back to the minister, willing herself not to think about how those wintry eyes had once blazed with hot need and breathtaking tenderness.

A few more words, another prayer, and it was done. As the last amen floated away on the sea breeze, mourners stood and began to talk softly among themselves. Sophie stayed seated, feeling numb, her limbs leaden, listless.

"Is it over?" Zoe asked, her lisp making the last word sound like "ov-oh."

She hugged the little girl close. "Yes, sugar. It's over."

"I don't want Mommy and Daddy to be in Heaven." The small voice nearly broke her heart.

"I know. Oh, honey, I know."

Someone with more experience around young children than she probably would have added something wise and comforting but Sophie drew a complete blank. She was still trying to figure out what to say when Sharon glided to them, weeping copiously. Not even her thick waterproof mascara could hold up under those conditions. Black splotches underlined her eyes, pooling in the wrinkles she fought so hard against.

"Oh, Sophie. Isn't this the most terrible thing that's ever happened? My poor girl. My poor baby girl. I never thought one of my girls would die before me. Oh, I don't know how I'll bear it.'' Sharon began to weep again and the barrel-chested man she'd brought along—another Earl, wasn't it?—handed her a handkerchief and patted her awkwardly on the shoulder.

Sophie should be more compassionate toward her mother. She knew it but still she fought a wave of resentment that even now Sharon couldn't stand to have anyone else be the center of attention. Not even her dead child or her suddenly orphaned grandchildren.

The instinct to flee was almost overwhelming. For one wild moment, Sophie wanted to grab her equipment and her suitcase and hop a plane to any destination, particularly one on the other side of the globe. A place where nobody knew her, where she could be just another anonymous face in the crowd hiding behind a camera lens.

Since she couldn't leave, at least she should be able to crawl into a bed somewhere—anywhere—and sleep for the next forty-eight hours until she lost this jet lag and could begin to cope with the storm of emotions that had buffeted her since Thomas's late-night phone call in Morocco.

Ten years ago she wouldn't have needed a phone call to tell her something had happened to Shelly. For most of their life, they had shared an invisible bond, one of those weird psychic twin connections that defied logic or words. When Shelly had broken her leg jumping off the swings in second grade, Sophie had crumpled to the floor of her classroom howling in pain. When Sophie had sliced a finger cutting vegetables in Home Ec, Shelly hadn't been able to finish a test in English class because her own finger throbbed too badly to write.

But that was all in the past. In the last ten years, Sophie had done everything she could to sever that bond, to put as much distance as possible between her and her twin, psychic or otherwise.

Obviously she had succeeded beyond her wildest dream. She hated that she had known nothing of the car accident that had killed Shelly—of that final terrible plunge off the soaring cliffs of Big Sur, of the impact so horrendous Peter had been flung from the Mercedes, his body dashed on the rocks below and then carried away by the violent sea.

Shelly had been dead three days before Thomas finally managed to learn what magazine she was on assignment for and could contact the photo editor and track her down.

Three days where she had been wandering from town to town, village to village. Eating, sleeping, laughing. Living her life just as always, with no clue her sister was gone.

She wanted to stand at that grave in this beautiful cemetery by the ocean and weep for the past and the physical and emotional chasm between them at the end.

"Can we go home now?"

Zoe's question wrenched at her heart, filled her mouth with shame. She was no better than Sharon. How could she stand here feeling so sorry for herself when these children had lost everything?

Home. She thought of Peter and Shelly's house on Seventeen Mile Drive, that huge estate in the gated Del Monte Forest that should have seemed elegant and cold.

For all its grandeur, Shelly had managed to make Seal Point feel like a home. That was just so Shelly. Her sister had plenty of experience building nests wherever they lived, from dingy apartments to run-down trailers and even the back seat of Sharon's old Toronado when they had spent a summer living out of it.

There were mourners to greet, polite conventions to follow, but she realized the children were close to the breaking point. They were her responsibility now and nothing else mattered.

"Yes, sugar. I'll take you home. Alison, are you ready?"

Her niece nodded tightly, and held on to Zach's hand. She led the little entourage toward her rental car. They had almost reached it when Thomas slipped away from his father's side and headed toward them.

"You're leaving?"

How did he make those two words sound like an accusation, a denunciation?

She straightened her shoulders. "The children are tired. I think they've had enough. They need to be in their comfort zone."

A muscle flexed in his jaw and he looked as if he wanted to say something, but he finally nodded. "I'll be along as soon as I can."

"That's not necessary," she answered coolly. "I'm sure the children and I will be fine."

"I'll see you at the house."

She didn't have the energy left to tell him he was the last person on earth she wanted to spend any time with today, so she just nodded and climbed into the rental car.

"It was a very nice service, don't you think? I mean, as far as these things go."

Tom glanced in the rearview mirror of the Jaguar. His father gazed silently out the window at the churning sea as they drove past Asilomar toward Country Club Gate. His Savile Row tie was slightly crooked, his silver hair a little mussed—things William Canfield never would have tolerated in better days. Maura McMurray sat beside him, solid and dependable as always, sympathy creasing her plump, no-nonsense features.

"Yes," Tom answered the nurse. "Peter would have been pleased to see so many people there."

Did that sound petty? he wondered. Yeah, probably, even though of course he didn't mean it that way. He sighed. Nobody could say his and Peter's relationship had been an easy one. He had loved his younger brother but they hadn't seen eye-to-eye on many things.

They had always wanted different things. Peter, like their father, had thrived on the influence and power of being one of the Canfields of Seal Point. He had loved the social scene, moving and shaking with the other leading families of the peninsula.

Tom had no patience for the thin, transparent superficiality of it all. Maybe that's one of the reasons he and his brother hadn't exactly gotten along. Peter—and William, for that matter—had never been able to understand the choices he had made with his life.

For all the good those choices had done him.

"I was glad to see Mrs. Canfield's sister made it in time for the funeral," Maura cut through his thoughts. "Although I have to admit it gave me quite a start when I first saw her sitting there with the children. Uncanny, the way the two of them look so much alike, isn't it?"

He made a noncommittal sound. It always surprised him when people made that observation. Certainly there were similarities between the sisters. They were twins, after all. They shared the same hair color, similar facial features, same slim, willowy build.

Both were strikingly beautiful, he had to admit, but his sister-in-law's appeal had been soft, gentle, like some impressionistic watercolor. Sophie, on the other hand, was wild and sensual—bold, vivid colors splashed onto textured canvas. Long tousled blond curls and sinful eyes and kiss-me lips.

"The children seemed taken with her, considering how seldom they've seen her."

"She stays connected with them," he murmured. Whatever else her failings, he had to give credit to Sophie for that. No matter where she traveled, she had always tried to stay in touch by phone or e-mail and she sent the children small gifts from all the exotic locales stamped on her passport.

"I suppose she'll be off again now."

"I don't know her plans but I'm sure she will." Sophie was the queen of the hit-and-run visit.

"Well, I hope she stays a while for the children. The poor dears will need all the family they can find right now. How awful for them to lose both their mother and father at once."

Maura's sympathy didn't seem to require a response. He glanced in the rearview mirror again and noticed his father playing with the power windows, rolling them up and down, up and down.

Maura competently distracted him with a pat on the hand and a small hand mirror she pulled from her bag, and William laughed and pulled a face at himself, his eyes scrunched up and his jaw sagging.

"Have you thought anymore about what you'll do now?" Maura asked.

Tom could feel tension grip his shoulders again with bony claws. Just thinking about all the choices he would have to make in the coming days made his chest ache.

"No," he answered tersely.

"I don't mean to push you. I would just like to know if I'll be needing to look for another position."

He frowned at the nurse. "Another position? Why on earth would you look for a new position?"

Maura cast a sidelong glance at his father, who was oblivious to their conversation as usual, then she met Thomas's gaze in the mirror. "You're going to have a big burden on your shoulders in the coming months, caring for the children and all and taking over your family's business concerns," she answered quietly. "I thought you might want to reconsider Mr. Canfield's living arrangements."

He didn't even want to *think* about this. Not today. "I'm not putting him in a nursing home, Maura. He'll stay at Seal Point as long as he can. That's his home, the place where he's most comfortable. You won't need to look for another position."

"It won't be easy for you, Lieutenant Canfield."

That grim fact had been crystal clear the minute his team had responded to that rescue call and he had recognized Peter's half-submerged Mercedes and Shelly's lifeless body still inside.

"I'll just have to try to do what's best for everyone." The trick was going to be figuring out what the hell that was.

The rest of the drive passed in silence and a few moments later they reached the curved iron gates of Seal Point, the home of his childhood and the place Peter and Shelly had lived with their children. With a press of the remote control, the gates slid soundlessly open.

Inside the house, he helped his father change out of his suit, unknotting his tie and unbuttoning his shirt as if William were a child.

"You're a good boy, Peter," his father said at one point, patting him awkwardly on the head as if he were ten years old again hitting a winning home run. Tom didn't bother to correct him. What was the use? Despite the funeral service, his father probably wouldn't even realize Peter—his golden son, the favorite—was gone.

Sometimes the injustice of it devastated him. His father, the brash and arrogant financier, was gone. In his place was this helpless, feeble man who couldn't remember how to dress himself but who had rare, heartbreaking moments of lucidity.

While Maura settled William with a bowl of soup and a sandwich from the self-contained kitchen attached to his rooms, Tom changed from his uniform into the Dockers and polo shirt he'd brought along, then went in search of the children.

He found them all in the main kitchen Shelly had modernized a few years ago for entertaining, with its marble countertops, six-burner stove and subzero refrigerator. They had changed clothes, too, the children into shorts and Sophie into a T-shirt that was a bit too small and a pair of worn jeans with fraying hems.

With her feet bare and all that glorious hair tied back into a ponytail, she should have looked young and innocent. Instead, she made him think of rainy afternoons and tangled sheets and slow, languid kisses.

How could part of him still be foolish enough to want her? Disgusted at his weakness, he clamped down on the unwilling desire and walked into the kitchen.

The children greeted him with none of their usual exuberance. Zoe and Zach sat at the breakfast bar watching cartoons on the kitchen television and Ali was pouring milk from the refrigerator into four glasses. Usually they dropped whatever they were doing and jumped all over him like a trio of howler monkeys but now all three just gave him subdued smiles that just about shattered his heart into tiny pieces.

Sophie's smile was just as subdued but several degrees cooler. It drooped at the corners, with exhaustion, he figured, since she had been traveling for days to make it in time for the funeral.

"Would you care for a sandwich?" she asked. "Mrs. Cope left cold cuts in the refrigerator but the kids were more in a PB&J mood. Nothing better than peanut butter and jelly when you've had a rough day like today."

He shook his head, absurdly touched that she was fixing comfort food for the children. "Maybe I'll fix one later."

"It's hard to work up much of an appetite, isn't it?"

"Yeah," he said grimly.

"How's William?"

He thought about giving his usual glib answer. *He's fine. Just fine. Thanks for asking.* But something in Sophie's green-eyed gaze—a bright glimmer of genuine concern—compelled him to honesty. "He doesn't really know what's going on, although Maura and I have both tried to explain about Peter and Shelly. In this case I suppose Alzheimer's can be a blessing."

She was quiet for a moment, then sent a look toward the children to see if they were paying attention to their conversation. "Shelly wrote me about his condition," she finally said. "I hadn't realized he had regressed so quickly. I'm sorry, Thomas."

He didn't know how to deal with the compassion in her eyes so he focused on something else, the circles under those eyes and the hollows under her high cheekbones. "Why don't you sleep? I'm here now."

She shook her head. "I doubt if I could. Maybe in a few more hours."

"You're going to fall over by then. Go on and rest."

Before she could voice that argument he could see her

gearing up for, the telephone rang in the kitchen. Thomas reached for it and heard her mother on the other end of the line.

"Hello, Sharon." In light of the loss they had all suffered, Thomas managed to conceal his dislike for the woman and handed the phone to Sophie.

If possible, Sophie's voice dropped several more degrees as she greeted her mother. Tom took over the sandwich-making while eavesdropping without shame.

Her expressive features had been one of the first things to captivate him all those years ago. She seemed a little more composed, a little more controlled ten years later, but he could still clearly see the tension rippling through her, the frustration simmering below the surface.

"No, I understand," Sophie said quietly. "Earl has a load to deliver and you've decided to cut your stay short and go with him. I didn't expect you to stick around long. No, that wasn't a dig, Sharon. Just an observation. Sure. Yes, I'll tell them. Goodbye."

Her mouth tightened for an instant as she hung up the phone but then her features smoothed out and she turned to the children. "Grandma Sharon is leaving this afternoon, kids. I'm sorry. But she says she'll be back through in a few months."

Ali and Zach barely looked up from the cartoon but Zoe gazed at her aunt, her eyes anxious. "Are you going, too, Aunt Sophie?"

Sophie must have caught that thin thread of fear in the little girl's voice. She paused in the process of opening a bag of chips, then set it down and swept Zoe into her arms. "Oh, no, honey. No! I'm not going anywhere, I promise."

Chapter 2

Thomas stared at her. How the hell could she look a child in the eye like that and utter such a bald-faced lie? Panacea or not, the children deserved the truth.

He waited just a few beats, until Zoe turned back to the TV then grabbed her arm. "Sophie, can you help me with something in the pantry?"

Those green eyes widened at the request and went even bigger when he yanked her into the six-foot by six-foot butler's pantry then slammed the door shut behind them. In such close quarters, he was instantly overwhelmed by the scent of her, exotic and sensual, like a rainy afternoon in the jungle, so he went on the offensive.

"Where the hell do you get off saying something like that?"

She frowned and jerked her arm away from him. "What did I say?"

"That you're not leaving."

"I'm *not* leaving."

His laughter was harsh. "That will be a first."

"The children need me, Tom, and I intend to be here for them."

"Until when? Your next assignment? Until you get the chance of a lifetime to shoot yaks in Nepal or whatever it is this time and off you go without giving a damn what you're leaving behind?"

Incredibly, unbelievably, hurt flashed for an instant in those wide green eyes but she shielded them quickly. "That's not going to happen."

"That's easy to say now. But what about a month from now? These are children, Sophie. Not pretty little toys you can put on the shelf when you're bored with them. They are children who have just suffered a terrible loss. Right now they need all the stability they can find until their world settles again. You really think you can give them that? You, of all people!"

Again that hurt flared in her eyes but she jutted her chin into the air in typical stubborn Sophie fashion. "What they need is *love* and I have more than enough of that to give them."

"Sometimes love is not enough."

"Isn't that the truth?" she muttered, an edge of bitterness to her voice.

He narrowed his gaze and studied her, trying to figure out if there was hidden meaning in her words. God knows, she had no reason to be bitter over their brief relationship. No, they hadn't had a relationship, he corrected himself. Just fledgling, unspoken emotions and one steamy encounter on the beach that could still make his heart race when he remembered it.

Then she ran away, for the first time but certainly not the last.

This time Sophie folded her arms over her chest, her chin still lifted defiantly. "I'm staying, Tom. The children need me. If you want me out of their lives, you're going to have to pry me out with a crowbar."

"Must I remind you, I am the executor of Peter's estate. His will specifically names me their guardian." He knew he sounded like a self-righteous ass but he didn't give a damn.

"And I have a letter from Shelly dated not two months ago where she asked me to care for her children if something happened to her."

Tom frowned, unease slithering through him like a moray eel cutting across the ocean's floor. Shelly had written Sophie? The timing seemed odd in the extreme. Why would a young, otherwise healthy woman write such a thing only weeks before her death? Did she have some impending premonition of danger?

"You can be as arrogant and domineering as usual," Sophie went on, heedless of the direction of his thoughts, "but that's not going to change my mind."

"The children are my legal responsibility," he repeated.

"They're as much my responsibility as yours, if not legally than at least morally. I don't care what Peter's will says. They are my nieces and nephew, and I love them. I'm not going to abandon them when they need me. Anyway, if I don't stay, who's going to care for them when you're out playing Rescue Ranger?"

Her scorn for his career shouldn't bother him but somehow it did. He should be used to it after ten years of fighting to live the life he wanted. Nobody understood his passion for his job. Not his father, not Peter. They had thought him crazy for turning his back on the family fortune to enlist in the military—in the plebeian Coast Guard, no less.

They didn't understand his passion for the service, for the unrivaled satisfaction of going after someone who needed help, the controls of his bird humming under his hands and adrenaline pumping like opium through his system.

That part of his life was over, he reminded himself. Peter's death had accomplished what his brother had never been able to do in life. "I'm putting in for a discharge," he murmured. "I'll be taking leave while the paperwork goes through."

Her expressive face softened instantly with sympathy. "Oh, Thomas."

He looked away from her pity, focusing on the rows of cans and bottles that the housekeeper kept in ruthless order inside the butler's pantry. "It's the best thing for everyone. The details of Peter's estate will keep me busy for weeks. In the meantime, I'm planning to hire someone to help Mrs. Cope with the children."

"For heaven's sake, you don't need to hire someone! I'm family. I love the children far more than some stranger you hire will."

For one crazy moment, the temptation to accept her help swamped him. With Sophie caring for the children, he might even be able to consider keeping his commission, just take a few months leave to handle the mess Peter had left behind at Canfield Investments.

He discarded the idea before it could take root. This was Sophie. Sophie, who had more stamps on her passport than Peter had neckties, who had made a successful name for herself traveling around the globe capturing whatever she found in her unique photographs.

She had inherited the restless gene that seemed to

have skipped over Shelly. Just like her mother, Sophie could never stand to stay in one place long enough to sprout.

And even if she did force herself to stay, he wasn't sure he wanted her caring for the children. After she left ten years ago and the hurt had begun to fade, he had realized the Sophie he had known had been flighty and reckless, irresponsible and selfish.

He'd meant what he said earlier. The children needed structure, stability, while they tried to cope with the loss of their parents. He couldn't risk their one safe harbor by introducing an alien species like Sophie Beaumont into the mix.

"Aunt Sophie? Uncle Tommy? Is everything okay?"

Ali's voice sounded from the other side of the pantry door, the worry in it adding another couple bricks of guilt to his load. "Just fine, Al. We're, uh, looking for more peanut butter."

"There's a whole jar out here." Suspicion coated her voice in a thin, crackly layer.

"Don't worry about it, Alison," Sophie said calmly. "We'll be out in a moment. We were just having a discussion we didn't want the twins to overhear."

"Are you sure?" Ali asked.

"Yeah, honey," he answered. "We're fine. Just go on back to the twins. We'll be right out."

Sophie opened the door as soon as they heard the girl walk away and he wondered if she was as uncomfortable in such close proximity as he was. "We don't have to fight about this, Thomas. Not today. Let's both sleep on it and give ourselves and the children a few days for things to settle down. We can talk about it again later."

As far as he was concerned, the matter was settled.

Whether she left this afternoon or a week from now, she would still leave. He had no doubt whatsoever.

The trick would be to make sure she didn't break the children's already fragile hearts when she went.

She could handle this, Sophie reminded herself hours later, up to her elbows in bathwater.

"Ow. That huwts, Aunt Sophie." Zoe made a face beneath her crown of suds. "Mommy doesn't go so hawd."

"I'm sorry. I'll try to take it easy." This was a little girl's head she was scrubbing, not a potato, Sophie reminded herself. This whole bath business was much harder than it appeared. Zoe insisted on everything just so—a water level exactly right, the precise temperature, her bath toys set out just where she wanted them.

She knew how vital it was for all of the children to keep to their usual routines as closely as possible, but she couldn't help comparing Zoe's elaborately complicated ritual with indigenous children she had photographed around the world who were perfectly content to perform their ablutions with a dirty puddle and a handful of leaves.

Maybe this wouldn't seem such an insurmountable challenge if she wasn't completely running on empty. She felt as wrung out as the washcloth Zoe was using and she wanted nothing more than to climb into that comfortable guest bed down the hall and collapse for a week.

But she could do this. She was strong, far stronger than Mr. Thomas Know-it-all Canfield believed her to be.

"Ow!" Zoe exclaimed again loudly and Sophie had to force herself to relax again.

"Almost done. Time to rinse."

"I don't like shampoo in my eyes," the little girl informed her matter-of-factly.

"I'll keep that in mind, honey."

She hoped Tom was having just as challenging a time with Zach in another of the estate's zillion bathrooms down the hall. After helping the nurse—Maura, she said her name was—settle his father for the evening, Tom had joined her to help with the children.

She found so much domesticity—the two of them working together at something so mundane and homey as putting the children to bed—unsettling. With any other man she probably wouldn't have thought twice about it, but this was Thomas. Thomas, who had kissed her and held her and treated her with such aching tenderness. Playing house with him like this was bound to unnerve her.

She jerked her attention away from that precarious road and back to Zoe. "There you go. That should do it."

"May I play for a while?"

It was past her bedtime but Sophie didn't have the heart to say no, not when Zoe had spent the day solemn and confused. For the first time all day she seemed like a little girl again instead of a silent, sad little waif.

"For a few moments." She rose on bones that creaked and complained with exhaustion, then made her way to the padded vanity bench across the bathroom. It didn't take long for the steam in the bathroom in combination with the comfortable seat to relax her stiff muscles. After a few moments she even felt her eyelids droop.

She jerked them open. She couldn't sleep! If Thomas came in and caught her dozing while Zoe splashed around amid so many possible water hazards, he would have all the proof he needed to show she was unfit to care for the children.

Not that he seemed to need any proof. He had made up his mind and changing it was going to be as tough as riding the Infierno Canyon rapids in Chile. She had to do her best to show him she could handle this, though. She couldn't abandon the children when they needed her.

Not the way she had abandoned Shelly.

The thought slithered into her mind and Sophie opened her eyes, all temptation to sleep forgotten as she bleakly watched the tendrils of steam curl through the room.

There it was. The truth she'd been hiding from all day. Not only was she compelled to stay and care for the children because she loved them and they needed her but because on some level she supposed she was trying to atone for the pain she had caused Shelly these last ten years.

She hadn't been there for her sister, but at least she would try for her sister's children.

Shelly never understood why Sophie had begun to freeze her out. She had never said anything, but Sophie had seen the hurt in her eyes during the few visits she'd made over the years, had heard the unasked questions in her voice every time they talked on the phone.

She should have tried to explain, damn it. About Peter and William and Thomas and that terrible night. In her frenzied rush to escape, though, she had decided it was best to stay quiet, to allow Shelly her illusions. Her sister had been happy with her new life here at Seal Point— deliriously happy, with her husband and her brand-new baby and this elegant home by the sea. How could she destroy that joyful light in Shelly's eyes by telling her about the den of vipers she had married into?

Now it was too late to explain anything to her sister. Grief and regret washed over her in cruel, unrelenting waves.

"Can we go to Point Lobos tomorrow and watch the otters?"

Sophie wiped at her eyes and found that her industrious niece had climbed out of the tub on her own and was wrapped in a towel, drying her hair. Chagrined at her own inattention, she hurried to help.

"That sounds fun." She cleared the remaining emotions from her voice. "We can talk about it with Ali and Zach and see what they want to do tomorrow."

"Talk about what?" Ali, her own hair wet from her shower, joined them in the bathroom wearing a pink cotton nightgown and matching robe.

"I want to go see the otters tomorrow."

"We just did that with Uncle Tommy two days ago."

"I want to go again." A stubborn light flickered in the little girl's eyes.

"I told her we would talk about it in the morning," Sophie said to head off the argument she sensed could easily brew.

Ali shrugged and went to work helping Zoe into her pajamas. The gesture made Sophie want to cry all over again. In just a few days without their parents, Ali had taken over mothering the twins. She was still a little girl, whose childhood had been snatched away from her abruptly and hideously.

While Sophie took over the task, she vowed a solemn oath to herself that she would do everything she could to restore that childhood.

"When will I go back to school, Aunt Sophie?"

Oh dear. She had so much to learn about being a parent. She hadn't given a single thought to them missing school. "Do you want to go back tomorrow?"

Ali's dimple flashed. "Tomorrow's Saturday."

She supposed she'd lost track after six connecting flights and a dozen time zones. "How about Monday, then?"

"Okay."

"Me, too," Zoe insisted. "Zach and me go to kindergarten. Miss Lewis is my teacher. She's pretty."

The three talked quietly about school and the girls' classes while Sophie brushed the tangles from Zoe's curly blond hair.

"You're all set now," she finally said. "Cleaner than a baby kitten."

"Will you read to us like Mommy does?" Zoe asked.

Sophie swallowed another damn lump in her throat. "Sure, honey."

"Mommy usually reads to us in her bed since it's bigger."

"Okay. Why don't you two find a book and I'll round up Zach and we can meet you there?"

She found Thomas and Zach in a bathroom down the hall. Tom's golf shirt was soaked and water covered the terra-cotta tile floor, she saw with amusement, but her nephew sported slicked-back hair and snazzy dinosaur pajamas.

"Whoa. Was there a tidal wave in here?"

Zach giggled. "I was showing Uncle Tommy how to dog paddle and some water splashed on the floor."

"And on your uncle, by the looks of it."

Tom made a wry face, which sent Zach giggling again. She had to admit, the sound was terribly sweet. "Aunt Sophie, did you know Uncle Tommy used to take a bath in this very tub when he was five? And he used to sleep in my room, too.''

The idea of Thomas as a five-year-old boy was just too difficult to fathom, especially with that soaked cotton showing every ripple of powerful, very grown-up muscles in his chest.

She sneaked a look at him under her lashes and couldn't help a quick intake of breath when she met his gaze, his blue eyes glittering with some expression she couldn't immediately identify.

''No, I didn't know that. Aren't you lucky that he lets you use it now?'' Her voice came out breathless as she answered Zach.

Just tired, she assured herself. Surely she wasn't still foolish enough to be attracted to the man. Not when she knew exactly how little Thomas Canfield thought of her.

''The girls and I are going to read a story before bed.'' She ignored the fresh surge of melancholy. ''Are you interested?''

''Yeah!''

''Okay, cowboy. We're reading in your parents' room.''

The fleeting animation on Zach's pointy little features slid away and he instantly sobered. *Oh, sweetheart.* Her heart ached all over again for the crushing loss these poor children had endured and she pulled him into her arms for a quick, comforting hug.

Unlike his sisters, Zach wasn't big on hugs, she was discovering. He pulled away after a moment and headed down the hall in search of Ali and Zoe. She watched his rounded shoulders for a moment, then turned back to find Thomas studying her again, his eyes gleaming in the bright fluorescent light of the bathroom.

''How are the girls?'' he asked.

"About the same as Zach. Fine one minute, on the verge of tears the next. It's going to take them a while to adjust to life without their parents."

"I think we're all going to need time to adjust."

She thought of the sudden, radical changes in his life from bachelor military pilot to father-figure businessman overnight. He must be close to overwhelmed but he seemed to be adjusting in typical competent Thomas fashion.

"Look, I can handle storytime so you can sleep," he began.

She shook her head. "I don't mind. I'm sure you have things to do."

"Only one or two million."

"Go on, then."

"Are you sure? You look exhausted."

She didn't know whether to be warmed by his concern or offended by the implication that she looked like hell. "I'll be fine. Once we're done reading, I'm sure I'll drop like a rock."

They stood for a moment in awkward silence, two people who were all but strangers, linked only by a brief, sketchy past and by their shared love for the three children. Still, they had made it through the first evening together without coming to blows, she thought. Maybe they could somehow figure out a way to make this complicated arrangement work.

She gave him a tentative smile, then turned and followed Zach down the hall.

Chapter 3

Some odd, discordant sound wrenched her from sleep. She blinked back to consciousness, to that first shocky awareness of her surroundings. It never took her long, probably because she'd spent her whole life waking up in different beds.

Narrow, lumpy cots in a seedy Russian hotel, grand ornately carved beds in a haunted Irish castle, communal woven mats on the floor of a grass hut in Samoa. She'd slept in them all and many, many more.

This time she was in a big, comfortable four-poster, the bed Shelly had shared with her husband.

She listened to try to determine what had awakened her but heard only soft, childish breathing. She was surrounded by warm shapes snuggled against her like puppies in a cardboard box, she realized.

How had that happened? She and the children had been reading, she remembered, some sweet, silly book about a kindergartner and her wild adventures.

Ali had taken a turn reading slowly and carefully, her brow wrinkled in concentration like Shelly's used to do.

Her sister would be so proud of her daughter. It was the last thought Sophie remembered.

Had she nodded off right in the middle of the story? She didn't doubt it, she'd been so exhausted. They all must have fallen asleep, exhausted by the ordeal of the day.

There were worse things in life than snuggling with three sleeping children. She smiled in the darkness and wiggled her toes.

Someone had covered them with a quilt, she discovered. Ali? she wondered, with a pang of regret for a child who carried the weight of too many responsibilities on her narrow shoulders.

It must have been. Who else?

She suddenly knew the answer. Not Ali. Tom. Somehow she knew without a doubt he was the one who had covered them.

Heat thrummed through her at the thought of Tom coming to look for the children and discovering them all nestled together. Of him standing by the bed, kissed by moonlight as he watched her sleep when she was vulnerable and exposed.

She shouldn't have this reaction to him, this trembling in her stomach, this slow surge of blood through her veins. He was just so damn beautiful, lean and dark and predatory like a panther she'd once been lucky enough to photograph in Punjab.

How were they ever going to make this work? In the darkness, all her doubts rushed back to pinch and poke at her. They both wanted custody of the children.

He would never let her take them away from here and

she wasn't sure she had the strength to stay here on the peninsula and deal with him day after day.

She sighed softly into the darkness and listened to the big house settle and creak around her. Shelly's house. Her sister had adored this huge, elegant villa with its dozen bedrooms and immaculate gardens. It wasn't the grandeur of the house that mattered. Shelly had never been like that—her twin would have been happy in a two-room trailer as long as she could stay in one place with the family she loved.

Their mother's wanderlust had always been much harder on Shelly than Sophie. Shelly wanted nothing more than to live in one place long enough to make friends, to put her name on the mailbox, to plant tulip bulbs and be there to see them break through the earth in the spring.

While Sharon worked as a cocktail waitress at some sleazy bar or other, Sophie and her sister had talked long into the night, spinning dreams about their futures.

Hers had been about finding fame and fortune, about saving the rain forest and seeing more of the world than just about every armpit of a town between the Atlantic and the Pacific.

All Shelly had ever wanted out of life was a man to love her, children to nurture, a home with a garden. She wanted to think her sister had found far more than she'd ever dared dream, here in this elegant, graceful home by the sea.

Too bad she had to take Peter Canfield as part of the package.

Her sister had been happy, though. She comforted herself with that knowledge. She had pressed—and pressed hard—to make sure Shelly was being treated right. Either her sister was a far better actress than she gave her credit for, or Shelly had never been unlucky enough to see the darker side of the man she married.

The side Sophie had seen.

A low, mournful wail cut through the night, jerking her out of her thoughts. The sound scraped along her nerves, raised gooseflesh on her arms. That's what had awakened her, she realized now. It was raw, unearthly, a supernatural kind of keening.

She rolled her eyes at herself. *You, who have slept with villagers telling tales of the* chupacabra *of Puerto Rico and the giant bat of Cameroon ought to know better than to let a little wind bother you.*

Still, her heart pounded an uneasy rhythm as she carefully picked her way through the maze of sleeping little bodies and padded to the sliding door that led to a small balcony overlooking the sea.

She unlocked it, disengaged the security system with the code Thomas had given her, and walked outside.

The night was cloudy and cool with a thick, ghostly mist curling up the cliffs through the coastal pine and cyprus. She leaned against the railing and peered into the darkness. All she could hear now was the crash and throb of the sea fifty feet below.

She heard nothing but the surf and her own breathing for several moments. Had she imagined it, then? She was about to chide herself for her overactive imagination and go inside to the children again when she heard it again, almost like a howl of pain.

Sophie peered into the darkness. Beyond the pool and back gardens, a long flight of wooden steps led down the steep slope to a small private beach. The sound seemed to have come from there. Clouds obscured the half moon but she thought she could just make out something huddled on the steps. A crouched silhouette.

The clouds shifted slightly and her gaze sharpened. It was a man out there wearing blue-striped pajamas, his shock of silver hair gleaming a pale, spectral white in the moonlight.

William! He must have wandered out of his apartment! Fear spurted through her. He could easily tumble down the steps, disoriented in the darkness. She paused for just an instant, then without another thought she hurried down the spiral ironwork stairs of the terrace and rushed across the wet grass, heedless of her bare feet.

When she reached him, William looked at her out of dazed eyes the same silver-blue as his son. The agonized grief on his face filled her with pity. The bitterness she had nurtured for so many years against this poor shell of a man seemed foolish now, so much wasted energy.

"I saw him," he mumbled. "Peter came to my room. Where's my son?"

He clutched at her T-shirt. "Shelly, where's my boy? They said he was dead but I know he's not."

Despite the shiver down her spine, she managed to gently disengage his hands. The poor man was delusional. He had mistaken her for Shelly—not so unusual since they were identical twins. "It's cold out here, Mr. Canfield. Let's get you back to bed."

After a moment he let her take his hand and lead him back to the house like a child. Just as they reached the door, Thomas burst through it, his hair messy and wild panic blazing in his eyes. He jerked to a stop when he saw them.

"What the hell are you doing out here with my father?"

Sophie bristled at his suspicious tone, his narrowed gaze, and slipped her hand from William's grasp. "I saw him at the top of the steps leading to the beach. I was afraid he would tumble down. But I suppose if you don't mind your father wandering around in the dark by himself, next time I see him I'll mind my own business.''

"That's impossible! There's no way in hell he could unlock the doors without tripping the alarm."

"You're right," she snapped. "I'm lying, you caught me. The truth is, I decided to wake up a frail old man and take him for a stroll around the garden at midnight, just for kicks."

"Stop fighting," William said suddenly, his voice sharp and clear. "Peter, I'm tired. I'm not in the mood for any more of your nonsense. I'm going to bed."

He walked into the house, leaving them gaping after him. Tom raked a hand through his dark hair, messing it even more. "I'm sorry, Sophie. I shouldn't have lashed out at you. It's just been a hell of a day. I fell asleep in the study and when I woke up, I went to check on him before going to bed and panicked when I found him gone."

"Don't worry about it."

"Look, I need to make sure he's settled back in bed. Will you wait here for me?"

She studied him. "No. My feet are freezing. But I'll wait for you in the kitchen."

She was heating milk on the stove when he came in ten minutes later looking tired and dispirited.

"Would you like some hot cocoa?" she asked.

He leaned against the work island. "I haven't had hot cocoa made the old-fashioned way since my mother died."

"It's much better this way." It had always been her and Shelly's comfort treat, something they shared on the nights when Sharon forgot to come home. She had been touched to find all the ingredients in a cupboard by the stove, as if Shelly used them often.

"It should only take a moment for the milk to heat. Is everything okay with your father?"

"Yes. He fell asleep as soon as I tucked him back in his bed. I can't for the life of me figure out how he got out. His room has a double lock and an alarm that's supposed to go off whenever the door is opened. He managed to work both locks and disengage the alarm. I suppose I'll have to figure out a better system."

"Does he do this often?"

"Not so much anymore. After he was first diagnosed, Peter and Shelly used to have to hide all the car keys or he would just take off and drive around all night. They wouldn't have the first idea where to find him. That's when we hired Maura to look after him."

"It must be terrible for him."

His shrug rippled the soft navy cotton of his shirt. "Strange as it seems, it's been a little easier the more his disease progresses. The first few years were tough but he doesn't really have an awareness anymore about what's happening to him."

He paused and turned his attention to her. "Look, I *am* sorry about snapping at you out there. I was acting on raw fear. I don't know what might have happened if you hadn't gone to his rescue. Thank you. It was lucky you happened to see him out there."

"I heard him first. He was weeping, Tom. Horrible, wrenching sobs. He thought I was Shelly and he said something about seeing Peter in his room. He was out looking for him."

"He thinks I'm Peter half the time. You heard him. Maura and I tried to explain about the accident but I don't know how much is getting through. Maybe it's better this way.''

How terrible it must be for Thomas to lose a little more of his father each day. With Peter's death, the responsibility of caring for his father now fell completely on his shoulders.

She longed to comfort him but didn't know how—and she wasn't sure if he would welcome her efforts anyway—so she busied herself with beating the cocoa to a froth.

When it was finished, she poured a mug for him and one for herself and the two of them sipped their hot drinks in silence for a few moments.

Thomas finally broke the silence. "I saw your work on Costa Rica in *Go!* magazine this month. You really brought the country and the people to life with your photos."

A compliment? From Thomas? Pleased and embarrassed—and unsure how to react to the unexpected comment—she focused on the murky cocoa in her mug with its swirls of lighter froth. "Thank you," she murmured. "It's a beautiful place. One of my favorites."

"I imagine you have many favorites."

She glanced up and found him watching her out of those silvery blue eyes. She managed to smile despite the little tug of awareness in her stomach. "It changes all the time. Usually, wherever I'm hanging my gear is my favorite."

"Do you ever get tired of the wandering life?"

Once more she wasn't sure how to answer him. She had found incredible success at her chosen field and she did love the thrill and adventure of discovering new places.

She enjoyed her life but she had never been able to

imagine herself spending the rest of it constantly moving around like Sharon, never content to spend more than a week or two in one zip code.

If she thought about the future at all, eventually she saw herself settling down, maybe working for a newspaper or teaching photography at a liberal arts college somewhere.

All that had changed with Thomas's late-night phone call to her hotel in Morocco. Now she had three children to think about.

"I've never known anything else," she finally answered his question. "But I'm going to learn for the children's sake."

Thomas wanted to argue with her again about her complete conviction that she was staying here to care for Ali and the twins but he bit back the words. Not now, when they had achieved this tentative, fragile peace here in the stillness of the night.

She had rescued his father and it seemed churlish to pay her back by more bickering. As she had said earlier in the evening, there would be time to discuss the future when things settled down.

Besides, the few hours of sleep she must have found snuggling in Peter and Shelly's room with the children didn't look to be enough. She gave a huge yawn suddenly, then blinked at him, a faint, appealing brush of color on her fair cheeks.

"Sorry. It's not the company, I promise."

"Don't worry about it. Get some rest. Come on, I'll walk up with you and help carry the children back to their own beds."

He followed her up the stairs, trying like hell not to notice the way the faded material of her jeans hugged her very shapely rear end. At Shelly and Peter's master suite, they found the children still cuddled together under the covers, Ali in the middle with a twin on either side.

He remembered how Sophie had looked sleeping peacefully surrounded by children when he had checked on them earlier in the evening. She had made a soft, innocent picture, her gold-blond hair tangled on the pillow in a wild, sensuous cloud.

"I don't think we should move them," Sophie said quietly at his side. "If they can find some comfort here together, I don't see the harm in it. I'll sleep over there on the sofa in case they should wake."

"There are a half-dozen guest rooms in this mausoleum where you would be far more comfortable."

"The sofa looks fine. I've slept on worse. Anyway, I'd hate for them to wake up and not know where to find me."

She smiled softly at him and for one astonishing moment, Thomas was overwhelmed by a wild urge to catch that smile with his mouth, to taste that smudge of cocoa at the corner of her lips.

He almost leaned forward but checked himself just in time, appalled at his idiocy where Sophie was concerned. "Good night," he muttered stiffly, then stalked down the hall.

No, it definitely wasn't going to work having her here. The sooner she figured that out, the better for both of them.

Chapter 4

His to-do list had taken on a life of its own.

Tom stared grimly down at the handwritten notes he had begun making soon after Peter's death. He was up to a half-dozen pages of tasks and counting. If he started this very moment and worked twenty-four hours a day, he was afraid it would still take him several weeks to tie up all his brother's loose ends.

During his three-year tenure as president and CEO of Canfield Investments, Peter had been fiercely aggressive, substantially expanding the family's financial interests. It was going to take Tom weeks to unravel all the tangled threads.

Weeks of paperwork and meetings and conference calls. He couldn't imagine anything worse.

Overwhelmed and disheartened by the job ahead of him, Tom gazed out the wide French doors of Peter's ground-floor office. In one of the peninsula's notoriously mercurial weather shifts, the unseasonable warmth of the last few days had vanished like the tide, leaving behind stormy gray skies and thick banks of coastal fog interspersed with heavy rains.

Even with the inclement weather, he couldn't deny the view through the rain-streaked window was still appealing. The gardens of Seal Point were lush year-round thanks to the efforts of Manny Reyes and his sons, who had taken care of the grounds as long as Thomas could remember.

In the steel-gray light and slanting rain, the flowers burned with saturated color—purples and blues and reds that waved on the stiff sea breeze. He had always found peace here, even when he was a wild, rebellious teenager butting heads constantly with his father.

He frowned suddenly as something disturbed the pleasing scene. What on earth? A parade of umbrellas darted through the gardens, bobbing and weaving through the plants.

He stared in disbelief. What was Sophie doing, dragging the children outside on such a grim day? It was definitely her, though, under a bright yellow umbrella and leading a precession of smaller umbrellas like a mother duck with her babies.

What kind of lunacy was she up to this time? He stood at the window frowning as he studied them. He had his answer soon enough when Sophie and her entourage trotted into the poolhouse and emerged a few moments later without their colorful umbrellas but wearing terrycloth robes and bathing suits.

He watched dumbstruck as all four of them—Sophie, Ali, Zach and Zoe—ran for the pool then leaped in, heedless of the rain pockmarking the surface.

She was crazy. She had to be.

Temperatures were probably only in the low fifties. It

was a better day for curling up with a good book by the fireplace than for splashing around in a swimming pool.

The pool was heated, he had to admit, at a comfortable eighty degrees. Regardless, he still couldn't imagine how she thought it would be good for the children to be outside in this rain. All he needed were three sick kids on his hands when Sophie decided to leave.

They were all going to catch their deaths.

This was just like Sophie, he fumed, thrusting open the door and marching outside.

She lived only for the moment and never bothered to think through the consequences of her actions, never thought about who would suffer those consequences.

While she had been flitting around the world taking her pictures, she likely had never given a single thought for her sister, or how Shelly might have worried herself sick sometimes about her twin traveling the globe alone.

It might be fine and dandy to take foolish risks when it was her own safety at stake. But she was supposed to be caring for three innocent children here—children who were ultimately his responsibility. He couldn't sit by and let them suffer because of her thoughtlessness.

He hadn't thought to grab an umbrella and the hard slap of the rain did nothing to cool his anger. It suddenly seemed terribly unfair of her to force him into the role of the bad guy. With each step, his temper flared higher until by the time he reached the pool, he was surprised steam wasn't sizzling off his skin with each raindrop.

The delighted smiles of the children when they saw him didn't help matters. They looked more light-hearted than he'd seen them all week. Instead of calming him, their obvious delight in this little adventure only added fuel to his ire.

"Hi, Uncle Tommy," Zoe called out. "Want to go swimming with us? It's fun!"

"No," he said shortly. "I think everybody needs to go back inside and dry out."

"But we just got in!" Zach protested. "We needed exercise. We've been cooped up all day. Sophie said so."

"You can exercise inside where it's warm and dry."

"We won't stay out here long," Sophie said. "Just long enough to burn off a little energy."

At her words he glanced over at her, treading water with Ali. Big mistake. She wore what on anyone else would probably be considered a perfectly respectable one-piece black bathing suit. But Sophie somehow made it look sleek and sensual. Even from the edge of the pool he could see her slim, curvy body straining the material of the suit.

If possible, he was even more attracted to her than he had been a decade ago, he realized with considerable chagrin.

She had been so young then, just coming into her beauty. The years had stamped strength and self-assurance onto her features, had turned a very lovely girl into a stunning woman.

He hated his own weakness where she was concerned. She had rejected him, made it quite clear she regretted their brief passion. Why else would she have left so suddenly?

And what kind of fool could still hunger for a woman who treated him like a pair of shoes she decided didn't fit after all?

"In case it's escaped your attention, it's raining."

She laughed. "Yes, I believe we're aware of that. If we weren't before, your drenched clothes probably would have given us a good clue. But we figured, what's a little rain when we were just going to get wet out here in the swimming pool anyway? Right, guys?''

The children agreed with her, Ali with a quiet nod and the twins with giggles he hadn't heard in days.

The sweetness of the sound made him bite back his sharp retort. He didn't want to fight with her in front of the children. They didn't need to see contention between the two people they had left. They were already uncertain, uneasy, about their future.

He gazed at them paddling in the water—if not happily then at least with more enthusiasm than they had shown toward anything else since their parents' deaths.

Part of him wanted to let them continue to splash and play, to work off some of their tangled emotions in the water. But he knew he couldn't jeopardize their health and safety just because they seemed to be having a good time.

He was trying his damnedest to think like a parent and he couldn't imagine his own parents ever letting him or Pete swim in the rain on a day like this.

"Time to get out." He used the same tone of voice he would with a recalcitrant subordinate under his command. "Everybody. Come on, time to get back into your robes and head inside. You can swim tomorrow if it stops raining."

Unused to that stern tone from him, the children looked to Sophie for guidance. Her gaze flickered toward them and then back to him, cool challenge in her eyes.

"We'll be out in a few moments. No more than fifteen, I promise."

Why did she have to be so difficult? This would be much easier if she didn't insist on being stubborn about having her way. Maybe it would be better if she left sooner rather than later. As long as she decided to stick around, he feared she would fight him at every turn.

He wanted to argue with her but he was hamstrung by the pleading in the children's eyes. Thomas groaned at himself. He was going to have to become a hell of a lot tougher if he was going to do a halfway decent job as a father-figure.

But maybe the week after their parents died wasn't the best time to be a hardass.

"Fifteen minutes, then you all need to go inside the house to get warm. Sophie, I would like to speak with you in the library when you're finished here."

The nod she gave him in reply was just as curt as his own voice had been.

"Are you sure you don't want to swim, Uncle Tommy?" Zach asked eagerly. "You're already wet. All you need is a swimming suit."

Despite his annoyance with Sophie, he managed a smile for his nephew. "Another time, bud. I have work to do."

The sooner Sophie decided to hit the road again, the better for all of them, he thought again as he marched back into the house, his shoes sloshing with every step.

Once she was flitting around the world with her cameras, he and the children would be able to establish a routine that didn't involve afternoon swims in the middle of a rainstorm or whatever other crazy scheme she might come up with.

And once she left, he should have no problem shaking this ridiculous attraction seething under his skin.

His temper still smoldered and hissed long after he changed into dry clothes and returned to the library Peter used as an office. He tried to immerse himself in the piles of work demanding his attention but he felt too prickly to make much headway.

Instead, he watched the four of them play in the pool through the rain-streaked glass. They seemed to be involved in a game of tag that had all of them grinning as they darted through the water.

Sophie seemed to be spending an inordinately long time being It, he noticed. She did little but pursue the children, her lithe body cutting through the water with grace and agility.

He couldn't hear them from inside but he was certain Ali and the twins were all laughing, genuinely enjoying themselves.

They were acting like children, for the first time since he'd had to break the news to them about Peter and Shelly. Despite his best efforts, since that day he hadn't been able to coax more than those heartbreaking, sad little half smiles out of them.

Just as the clock ticked down the fifteen minutes she had said they would remain outside, he watched her gather the children around and say something to them, then the four of them climbed out of the pool and rushed toward the poolhouse for robes and umbrellas.

A few moments later they headed for the house, their faces bright and rosy—from the cold or the exercise, he couldn't tell.

With a frown, Thomas turned back to the papers spread across the desk and pretended to concentrate while the ormolu clock on the mantel ticked down the moments.

Thirty-three minutes later—not that he was counting or anything—a knock sounded at the door.

Without waiting for a reply, Sophie opened it and walked into the office dressed in jeans and a soft rose-colored sweater, her hair captured in a still-damp ponytail.

His reaction to her was as instant and powerful as it was unwelcome.

She made a big show of giving an elaborate curtsy. "I believe you rang for me, my lord."

He glared at her pert tone. That was exactly her problem. Sophie thought she could laugh her way through life, that the world was one big adventure created only for her.

Ten years ago she had glowed with enthusiasm for life, wanting to taste every delicious morsel of excitement the world had to offer. She had been hungry to explore, to embrace, to experience.

Had he been just another of those little adventures of hers? The thought didn't sit well with him. Not well at all.

"I'd like to know something. Can you tell me how in the hell you have survived on your own all these years with absolutely not one smidgeon of anything resembling common sense?"

She raised an eyebrow. "Dumb luck?"

"I believe it. What were you thinking, Sophie?"

With complete disregard for the paperwork spread across it, she perched on the edge of the desk, far too close for his comfort.

He was furious with himself for the instinctive way he leaned back—and even more so when he thought he saw a hint of amusement play at the corner of her mouth, as if she enjoyed making him uncomfortable.

"I'm assuming this lecture has to do with our little swim party."

"This has to do with you not giving a thought to the consequences of your actions, as usual. This has to do with the complete irresponsibility of taking three young children out in a cold, hard rain to swim without giving a single thought to their health and welfare.''

''Are you finished?'' she asked, her voice icy.

He paused long enough to look at her and realized with some shock that she was angry, too. He had never seen her mad. Amused, entranced, aroused, but never mad.

He sat back in Peter's chair. ''Not even close.''

''Too bad. You've had your say. Now I get a turn. You're completely wrong, Thomas. Believe it or not, I did consider the wisdom of taking them out in the rain and I did consider the possibility they might catch cold.''

''But you took the risk anyway.''

''I took the risk. And it was worth every moment. You were watching them. I saw you in here standing at the window. You must have seen the same thing I did. They were laughing. Smiling and laughing and behaving like children instead of quiet little wraiths.''

He couldn't deny the truth of her words. ''Yes, I saw them. But they won't be laughing when they all are sick in bed with pneumonia. What will you do if they get sick?''

''I'll make them chicken soup and tuck them into their beds and read them every story in the house. But I'd rather see them laugh and splash and catch cold than shrivel away into quiet, spiritless little mice.''

All right, so maybe he had been a little more angry than the situation demanded. Perhaps she hadn't been completely irresponsible after all. He sighed heavily, reluctant to admit he might have overreacted. ''Couldn't you have found another way to raise their spirits?''

''Maybe. But that was the first thing that came to me. They were restless and upset this morning. I don't know if it was the rain or reality finally sinking in that Peter and Shelly are truly gone but they needed something to distract them, some way to work off that snarl of emotions. Swimming seemed like a good idea. But perhaps next time I'll try to think of something else. Jumping on the beds, maybe, or timing which of us can slide down the bannister the fastest.''

He shuddered, imagining the mayhem she could wreak if let loose. Sophie only gave one of those low, sexy laughs of hers he remembered so well, one of those laughs that always used to strum through him.

"I'm doing my best, Tom," she said, sobering. "I'm sorry for everyone's sake that I'm not better at this, that I don't really know what I'm doing with the children. But I am trying."

For how long?

The question burned in his mind but he didn't voice it. How long before she packed up her gear and caught a plane away from Seal Point, leaving the children with yet another loss to struggle through?

He couldn't ask, not when she gazed at him with such earnest entreaty in her green eyes.

"Fine," he said tersely. "But no more swimming in the middle of a rainstorm."

She gave him a mock salute. "Aye-aye, captain."

"That's lieutenant."

"Right. Sorry." She smiled and for a moment the usual tension that writhed between them was gone.

He wanted to bask in that smile for a while and forget the past and all his unanswered questions.

But he also wanted to think he wasn't quite the idiot he'd been a decade ago. He forced himself to lean back farther in Peter's leather chair. "How are the children now?" he asked with studied casualness.

"Grand. At least they were when I left them. Mrs. Cope popped a big batch of buttery popcorn and they're eating it while they watch an old movie. Swaddled in plenty of warm blankets, I might add."

"Now that sounds like just the thing for a stormy Saturday afternoon like this one."

She studied him for a moment and he wondered if she could tell the effort it cost him to pretend indifference to her. "Why don't you join us, Tom? The children would be thrilled to make room for you on the couch. You look as if you could use a break."

Was it that obvious how much he dreaded dealing with the thousand details awaiting his attention? Her invitation held undeniable appeal. It was far too tempting.

He glanced at the small mountain range of paperwork. "Thanks, but I've got to put some order to at least some of this chaos by Monday when I'm meeting with Peter's attorney."

She straightened from the desk, her lithe body unfurling like one of Manny Reyes's flowers. "Okay. But we'll save some popcorn for you if you change your mind."

To his vast relief, she headed for the door.

"Thanks," he said before she reached it. "Oh, and I'm, uh, sorry for jumping on you like that earlier."

Her eyebrows lifted a little at his apology, then she offered him another swift, dazzling smile and walked out.

He gazed at the closed door for a long time after she left. For a moment there, she had reminded him so painfully of the woman he had known a decade ago. The girl, really. She hadn't been much more than that, barely twenty.

He had been twenty-four, new to the Coast Guard and

stationed in Juneau, Alaska. His two-week furlough happened to coincide with Ali's birth so he'd flown to the peninsula to meet his new niece and spend a few days at Seal Point.

He had expected a quiet, uneventful trip home.

Instead, he'd found Sophie and had fallen for her like a Sikorsky with a bent rotor.

He hadn't expected the instant and fierce attraction between him and the sister of his kid brother's sweet new wife. But she had been completely irresistible—fresh and exuberant and intoxicating.

He had fought his attraction to her for days, reluctant to start what he knew could only be a fling. What else could it have been? She lived in New York, he'd been stationed in Alaska. Besides the five thousand miles between them, he wasn't looking for a relationship, especially not with a twenty-year-old kid just beginning to explore the world.

But then he'd kissed her on a dawn-drenched cliff overlooking the Pacific and all the arguments he had spent days constructing collapsed like a sandcastle at high tide.

He had fallen for her hard, hadn't been able to help himself.

He thought she had returned his feelings. She had kissed him and laughed with him and shared her dreams, her soul, her body.

And then she had left him without a word, only hours after they made love for the first and only time.

Tom jerked his mind away from that particular memory, of silky skin and soft sighs and eager kisses. He didn't need to dwell on something so transitory, so ephemeral.

Their moments together had been one tiny slice of

time. Something that obviously had little meaning to her or she wouldn't have walked away so abruptly or offered excuse after excuse not to talk to him when he tried to contact her after she returned to New York.

He should be doing his best to keep a safe emotional distance between them, not dredging through the murky waters of their past.

It wouldn't be easy, he was very much afraid. Not when something about Sophie Beaumont still called to him as strongly as ever.

Chapter 5

This wasn't a bad way to spend a few hours.

Sophie leaned back in one of the deep leather sofas in the media room of Seal Point and tucked a brightly patterned quilt around Zoe. The child nestled closer on her lap but didn't take her eyes off the animated Disney video showing on the huge plasma-screen TV.

The controversial swim had accomplished exactly what Sophie had hoped. The physical activity seemed to have relieved the restlessness that had made the children cranky and out of sorts.

Now they appeared relaxed and snug and were even laughing at some of the funnier bits of the movie.

As soon as she returned from speaking with Tom, Zoe had crawled into her lap while Ali and Zach had claimed the floor, propped on a mountain of pillows they'd pulled from a corner of the room.

The media room was the perfect retreat and looked as if it could easily accommodate a crowd of a dozen or more. The couch she and Zoe used was one of four arranged at angles on the sloped floor so occupants all had a clear view of the screen.

Shelly had designed the media room, Sophie was sure of it. It was exactly her twin's style—cozy and comfortable and warm. A place designed for family and friends to enjoy time together.

She could feel her sister's presence here in the plump pillows and the campy old movie posters framed on the wall and the fountain drink dispenser near the back wall.

Zoe cuddled closer and Sophie smiled and pressed a kiss to the little girl's blond curls. Not a bad way to spend a few hours at all.

How often had Shelly done this with her children? she wondered. Snuggled with them and watched a movie on a rainy evening? It seemed routine enough to the children that she had to assume it had been a frequent enough occurrence.

Peter had enjoyed the Monterey social scene, she knew. But she imagined Shelly would have been much happier spending her evenings here with her children than out at cocktail parties and gallery openings.

She sighed, wondering how she would ever nurture the children as their mother had, as they deserved.

Shelly had been a natural at the whole motherhood thing. All she had ever wanted was a home and children of her own.

When they were kids, she had gone everywhere with a pitiful little ragtag cloth doll Sharon had picked up at a yard sale. Shelly would have even tried to slip it into her backpack to take to school if Sophie hadn't caught her and talked her out of it.

That part of her sister had baffled her, she had to admit, since it was one she definitely hadn't shared. Sophie hadn't been the least interested in dolls or playing house or dressing up. She preferred climbing trees or roller-skating or lying on her stomach in the grass and watching a colony of ants bustle across a summer sidewalk.

She remembered thinking when they were kids how odd it was that she and Shelly could look so much alike but be so very different in their personalities.

The one passion they both shared was books. No matter where Sharon dragged them, the first thing she and her sister did was find a library and apply for brand-new cards.

She supposed a therapist would easily decipher that by escaping into books, both girls were looking for any way they could find to cope with the uncertainty and chaos of life with Sharon.

Maybe that's why the idea of parenting three young, needy children terrified her so much, why she'd never really even considered having children of her own.

What did she know about being a loving mother? Her only frame of reference for a parent-child dynamic had been with Sharon. Not exactly the most healthy of relationships. She couldn't bear the idea of ever treating a child with the kind of careless negligence she and her sister had endured.

She didn't necessarily have to repeat old patterns, she reminded herself. Shelly hadn't taken after their mother—she had found her own way of parenting.

And though Sophie hadn't understood this part of her sister—this maternal, nurturing side—with this beautiful child warm and soft in her arms, she was beginning to get a glimpse into Shelly's heart. In the past few days she had discovered a sweet kind of peace surrounding her when she was with the children, settling into her soul.

She could do this, could take over where Shelly had left off. It would be the biggest challenge of her life but she would do her very best for Ali and the twins. No matter what Tom thought of her.

Ah, Thomas. She sighed loudly enough that Zoe sent her a chiding look for distracting her from the movie.

"Sorry," Sophie whispered. She tried to focus on the screen but her thoughts inevitably drifted back to him like loose kelp finding the shore. As foolish and futile as she knew her attraction to him was, she couldn't seem to control it.

She couldn't believe that even with an entire decade and a million frequent flier miles between them, there was still *something*—some undefinable, inexplicable spark—that buzzed and popped between them whenever they were together.

She had been intrigued by the thrilling power of it ten years ago when she had been too young and foolish to know any better. Now she was terrified by it.

He was older now and far more potent to her psyche and she had a feeling he could leave her heart broken and bloody if she let him.

As if conjured by her thoughts, the door suddenly opened and Thomas walked into the media room.

"Hi, Uncle Tommy," Zach said from the floor. "Did you come to watch the movie?"

He grinned down at his nephew and Sophie groaned at her reaction, wondering how something as inconsequential as a simple smile toward a little boy could send her stomach dipping and fluttering like a bumpy landing on a 747.

"I tried as long as I could but I finally couldn't resist the smell of that yummy popcorn. Is there any left?"

Sophie held out the huge bowl Mrs. Cope had popped. "Plenty. Sit down and watch."

She expected him to take one of the other three couches in the room but instead he surprised her by sitting next to her and Zoe. She swallowed hard, trying fiercely not to notice the distinctive, tantalizing scent of him that reached her even through the buttery aroma of the popcorn.

He favored the same aftershave he had used a decade ago, some undoubtedly expensive mix of leather, citrus and some other woodsy scent she couldn't identify. Juniper, maybe, or cedar. She wasn't any good at figuring out fragrances; she only knew that once she had smelled that same cologne in a Nice market and had stood at that stall for what felt like hours, her nose in the vial and her mind reliving every incredible second on that warm Seal Point beach with him.

She wanted to close her eyes and just savor that smell and the heat of him next to her but she forced herself to keep them rigidly open.

After a moment, Zoe abandoned her and climbed into her uncle's lap. He drew her close and settled deeper into the sofa while Sophie tried not to let it bother her.

The children naturally felt closer to Tom—he lived in the area and saw them far more frequently than she did. They shared a bond she would have to earn. Still, it smarted, she had to admit.

With effort, she put away her hurt and tried to focus on the movie. After a few moments she reached for a handful of popcorn in the bowl next to her on the couch. By some quirk of fate, Tom reached for a handful of his own at exactly the same time.

Their fingers brushed inside the bowl and a quick

spark sizzled between them. Her gaze flew to his and she found him watching her, raw hunger in his eyes.

She had a sudden, almost painful awareness of her blood pulsing through her veins, of her lungs slowly working to draw air, of her body stirring to life.

She wasn't sure how long her gaze stayed locked with his, the movie and the popcorn and the children forgotten. Suddenly she was twenty again, young and foolish, swallowed up by that wild, terrible flush of first love.

Some loud noise in the movie jerked her back to the present and her surroundings and she quickly looked back at the screen with a fierce attempt at concentration that she was sure fooled no one.

"Aunt Sophie, look! I went all the way to the end of the driveway and didn't fall down once!"

She smiled at the pride in Zach's voice. "You're doing great! I knew you could do it."

"And me too," Zoe chimed in, still tightly clutching Sophie's hand as if she'd be sucked away by the lightest of breezes if she dared let go. "I can skate, too."

Sophie wobbled a little on the pair of inline skates she had found jumbled together in a box tucked into a closet of the children's big playroom. "You're both fantastic. I would have fallen on my behind a dozen times if you weren't holding me up."

Zoe squeezed her hand even more tightly, nearly cutting off her circulation. "I won't let go, I promise."

"Good." Sophie tried not to wince at her aching fingers and headed back down the driveway.

Though the weather was still cool, the four of them were enjoying a temporary break in the clouds to play on the curved asphalt driveway at Seal Point. It was the perfect surface for learning to skate, as silky smooth as sea-polished stone.

All day she had tried to keep them busy with one activity after another. She was learning distraction was important to the children in these first painful days of trying to cope with the loss of their parents.

Even though their grief was always present—like the low murmur of the sea below them through the trees— the children were beginning to smile a little more often. It would be a long, painful process, she knew, but they were headed on the right path.

She watched Zach and Ali skate ahead of them, their arms waving wildly to help them keep their balance. She would have liked to photograph all of them right here, with their faces rosy and the afternoon sun slanting through the coastal pines to brush their hair gold.

She was debating whether she was up to the ordeal of taking off the skates in order to fetch her gear from upstairs when Zach and Ali switched directions and skated over to them.

"I wish Uncle Tommy could see me." Zach glanced toward the house. "I should tell him to come out and play with us."

"No," Sophie said quickly. "I'm sure he's very busy. Maybe after we practice a little more we can show him how we're doing."

She absolutely did *not* want Thomas to come outside. Since the evening before and those intense few moments with the popcorn, she had been excruciatingly careful to keep as much distance as possible between them. She had sat through the rest of the movie in a still, wary silence, almost afraid to breathe for fear of touching him again and sparking more of those terrifying sensations.

He seemed just as cautious. As soon as the closing

credits started to roll, he had left the room quickly with a kiss and hug for each of the children and a strained smile for her.

Since then she had scarcely seen him. They had passed briefly in the kitchen at breakfast but he had been with William and she had been busy with the children and they'd done little more than exchange hellos.

This was all just so terribly awkward, she thought as she led her little entourage on another pass toward Seal Point's imposing iron gates. She wasn't sure of her place here, how to behave, what to do.

If she and Tom had no history between them, things would be so much less complicated. They would simply be two people whose only link was the marriage of their respective siblings, and through that, these beautiful children.

But she felt as if the past had imprinted its memory on every interaction she had with him. She found herself remembering things she had tried hard to suppress for a decade and she couldn't help but wonder how much *he* remembered of their time together.

Did he also think of cool sand and sweet kisses and tangled bodies while the surf murmured around them? Or had their time together just been a regrettable period in his life? One he would prefer to forget?

She couldn't read much in those silver-blue eyes of his. He was an expert at shielding his emotions.

If she hadn't been distracted by her thoughts, she might have been able to avoid the catastrophe.

Just as they reached the gates, Zoe's skate hit a small rock on the driveway. Off balance by it, she started to fall, tugging Sophie down with her. Sophie wobbled and did her best to stay upright with fifty pounds of force pulling her down. She might have succeeded if Ali hadn't rushed to help them both from falling. Somehow one of her wheels caught on Sophie's.

Her fledgling skills just weren't enough to keep Sophie vertical. The skates went one way, she went another, and the hard asphalt driveway did nothing to cushion her fall.

The breath whooshed out of her as Ali landed on top of her. For several seconds the three of them—Zoe, Ali and Sophie—lay tangled together.

"Are you guys okay?" Zach skated closer to ask.

Still breathless, Sophie managed a nod just as Zach's skate caught on the same blasted pebble that had been his twin's undoing. His downfall was almost an exact duplicate of Zoe's. He teetered for a moment and tried to maintain his balance then crash-landed on the pile of giggling females just as Sophie saw a dark sedan pull to a stop outside the gates.

A woman in her mid-thirties with a short wispy haircut and a severely cut suit climbed out of the driver's side door.

"Is everyone all right?" she asked through the gate, sliding sunglasses atop her dark hair.

Sophie gave an embarrassed laugh. "I think so. No broken bones, right guys?"

The children shook their heads, suddenly shy around a stranger. Hanging on to the gate, Sophie pulled herself up then helped first Ali and the twins to their feet before she turned to face the woman again.

Their visitor had been joined by a man who had emerged from the passenger side of the sedan, Sophie noted. He was younger than the woman by perhaps a half-dozen years. Despite their different coloring—he was beach-boy blond to her darker hair and features—

he wore a similar dark suit and had the same no-nonsense look to him.

"You must be Shelly Canfield's sister," the woman
said. "I'm sorry for staring. I'm sure you hear this often
but I must say, the resemblance is startling."

"We are...were identical twins." Would this grief
that stabbed at her whenever she thought of her sister
ever fade? "I'm Sophie Beaumont. Were you friends of
Shelly or Peter?"

Even as she asked the question, somehow she knew
they weren't. Peter was a snob when it came to his
friends and for some reason she doubted these two
would meet his elitist criteria.

"We're with the Federal Bureau of Investigation, Ms.
Beaumont." The woman pulled a small leather case
from her jacket pocket and flashed a badge that reflected
the sunlight with a sharp glare. "I'm Special Agent Candace Herrera and this is my partner, Special Agent Tate
Washburn."

FBI agents? What would the FBI be doing here? Before she had a chance to ask, she caught sight of the
children's subdued faces.

Ali had reached out to hold Zoe's hand and Zach was
clutching the edge of Sophie's shirt like it was a security
blanket. They didn't need another reminder that their
world had suddenly become a grim and frightening
place, she realized.

"I'm not sure how to work the gate from out here,"
she said quickly. "If you'll wait for a moment, I'll take
the children inside and buzz you through from there."

"Certainly," the younger agent said with a friendly
smile and what she suspected was more than professional courtesy in eyes the same pure blue of the Car-
ibbean. "We don't mind waiting."

No one fell on the way inside the house. Her mind whirling with questions, Sophie opened the door closest to the kitchen and ushered the children inside.

"Why don't you all find Mrs. Cope for a snack?" she suggested.

Zoe's eyes widened. "Aunt Sophie, we're not allowed to skate inside. We'll get in trouble."

"I know. You can take your skates off right here."

While the twins sat on the ground and began unbuckling their skates, Sophie pulled their older sister aside. "Ali, tell Mrs. Cope you're starving from all that skating. I'm sure she'll fix you something yummy and I'll join you in a few moments."

"Aunt Sophie," the older girl said, her voice low so her siblings didn't overhear, "Do you think they're here to talk about the accident?"

Sophie forced a reassuring smile. "I don't know, honey. I won't know that until I talk to them."

She didn't add that she had no idea why the FBI had any interest in a tragic accident on Highway 1. She squeezed Ali's fingers. "You don't need to worry about it. That's my department. Mine and your uncle's. You just go have a snack with your brother and sister, okay?"

After a moment, Ali nodded and Sophie pushed the button to open the security gate for the FBI agents. While they were driving their car around, she slipped off her skates quickly and shoved her feet into her tennis shoes then rushed through the house to open the front door for them.

The nondescript sedan pulled up in front of the house just as she reached the door and a few moments later the two agents joined her at the top of the wide flagstone steps.

"Come in." She led them to an elegant receiving

room off the entryway and gestured for them to be seated.

"How can I help you?"

Agent Herrera leaned forward with a polite smile. "Actually, Ms. Beaumont, we'd like to speak with William Canfield."

"William?" Sophie didn't quite manage to hide her surprise. "You're sure you wanted to talk to William?"

"Yes. Is he available?"

That depended on the way one defined the word "available." Since she wasn't exactly sure how much Tom wanted to reveal to outsiders about his father's condition, she hedged. "Mr. Canfield is…not taking visitors, Ms. Herrera. Perhaps his son could help you. His oldest son Thomas is handling the family's business concerns."

The two agents exchanged a look, then Agent Herrera nodded. "Is he available, then?"

"I don't precisely know. I haven't seen him for a while—it's a rather large house, as you can see." She managed a small, polite smile. "I'll certainly look for him, though. In the meantime, would either of you care for something to drink?"

Both declined, so Sophie quickly went in search of Tom. She found him in the first place she looked, exactly where he seemed to be spending most of his time, in Peter's office.

The door was open. When she peered through, she saw him seated behind his brother's desk poring through a pile of papers in his hand. Tight lines of concentration feathered out between his brows and a vague air of restlessness surrounded him.

He didn't appear to be enjoying himself. But then, he

probably wouldn't consider a visit from the FBI exactly entertaining, either.

Reluctantly, she stepped into the room. He didn't appear to notice, too engrossed in the paperwork, so she cleared her throat. He looked up in surprise and she thought for a moment his eyes gleamed with a quick, raw desire before he blinked it away.

"Tom," she began, a little breathlessly. "I'm sorry to disturb you."

"Are the children all right?"

"Yes. They're fine. I came to tell you that you have visitors. Would you like me to send them back here?"

His features tightened. "I'm not really in the mood for a condolence call. Can you make up some excuse for me?"

"It's not a condolence call." She paused, strangely reluctant to add another burden to his already heavy load.

"Who is it, then?" Impatience threaded through his voice like mist curling off the sea.

"Tom, they're FBI agents."

Chapter 6

For a few seconds, Thomas thought maybe the headache pounding through his skull had made him hear incorrectly. But Sophie still stood in the doorway, her normally unflappable demeanor decidedly flapped. Her green eyes were wide and uneasy and her shoulders were tight with tension.

"I don't understand. Why would the FBI want to talk to me?"

"They originally wanted to talk to your father. I told them he wasn't available. I'm sorry—I didn't know how much information you wanted me to give out about his condition."

Peter was the one who had insisted on keeping William's condition a secret, who had hidden him away in seclusion here at Seal Point.

Only a few very close friends knew just how far William's condition had deteriorated. Peter had wanted to maintain a perfect front to the world, to conceal anything that might reflect poorly on the old and respected Canfield name.

Tom hadn't agreed. He knew that no matter how careful they all were, sooner or later word would slip out. It was impossible to keep a secret on the peninsula. He had always figured it would be far better to be open and upfront with everyone about William's disease.

But Peter seemed to think public disclosure would erode shareholder confidence in the company. Tom thought his younger brother was paranoid but he decided it wasn't worth the energy to fight about it, especially since Peter and Shelly had agreed to take on the bulk of the responsibility for William's care. Well, Shelly had, anyway.

He supposed now that Pete was gone, he could run an ad in the damn newspaper if he wanted. William's care was *his* responsibility, just like everything else.

His headache racheted up a notch. ''Where are the FBI agents?''

''I settled them in the small room off the entry.''

He nodded and rose from the desk, then headed with Sophie toward the room his mother had always called the visitor's salon.

As they made their way through the sprawling house, he was conscious, as always, of her fluid grace. She moved like a dancer, like a waterfall trickling over stone. She always had, even when she was just a young woman barely aware of her body.

Back then he could have watched her simply walk across a room for hours, just savoring the poetry in her movements.

He caught the direction of his thoughts and had to restrain himself from grinding his back teeth. The poetry of her movements. What the hell was the matter with

him? He had far too many things on his plate to waste
any time remembering how Sophie Beaumont used to
turn him on just watching her loose-limbed walk.

Or how she still did.

He had to do something about this unwilling attraction
for her. What that might be, he didn't have the first idea
but he knew he was going to have to think of something
fast.

He was almost relieved when they reached the room
where the FBI agents waited.

Sophie paused outside the door. "I'd better go find
the children. They'll be finishing their snack with Mrs.
Cope soon."

He wasn't sure what compelled him to place a re-
straining hand on her arm. "No, stay. I'm sure the kids
are fine in the kitchen for a few moments. To be honest,
I have a feeling I'm going to need some moral support."

She gave him an odd look but shrugged and followed
him into the room. A man and a woman were seated on
a sofa but both rose when he and Sophie entered. He
had a quick impression of intelligence and cool com-
petence before the female agent spoke.

"Lieutenant Canfield?"

"Yes. I'm Tom Canfield."

"Peter Canfield's brother?"

"Yes."

Her gaze shifted briefly to the other man then the female agent spoke again. "I'm Special Agent Candace
Herrera and this is my partner Special Agent Tate Washburn."

"Please sit down." They complied and Tom gestured
to an armchair in the room for Sophie then took a matching chair next to it. When everyone seemed to be settled,
he turned back to the FBI agents. "Can you tell me what

this is about? To be honest, I'm having a tough time figuring out why the Feds would have any interest in what amounts to a family tragedy. Last I heard, the California Highway Patrol is the investigating agency into the accident that killed my brother and sister-in-law.''

''We're very sorry for your loss,'' Agent Washburn said promptly. ''We're not actually here about the accident, although we are assisting in that investigation.''

''Assisting how?''

Again, Tom was aware of an awkward pause. ''This is difficult, Lieutenant Canfield,'' Agent Herrera finally said.

''I guarantee, whatever you have to tell us can't be any more difficult than the week we've just been through. It hasn't been an easy time for any of us.''

As if remembering her presence, Agent Herrera glanced at Sophie then back at him, her dark eyes expressionless. ''Actually, would it be possible to speak with you in private, lieutenant?''

Sophie immediately started to rise but he reached out and placed a hand on her arm, conscious of the silky warmth of her skin even through his mounting tension. ''That won't be necessary. Ms. Beaumont has the same interest in anything to do with the accident that killed Peter and Shelly as I do. She has as much right to hear what you have to say.''

Sophie's eyes widened with surprise at his words but the FBI agent merely nodded. ''Right. That's certainly your choice. I'll get straight to the point then. Do you know a man named Walter Marlowe?''

''Of course. He was a close friend of my father's as well as chief financial officer, second-in-command at Canfield for years. I know Peter trusted him implicitly.

His death was a severe blow to my brother and to the entire company.''

Dealing with the tangled mess Peter had left of things wouldn't be nearly as challenging if Walter were still around to help him. He had already come to sorely miss the man's counsel.

"Are you aware of the circumstances of his death?'' Herrera asked.

"I was on a training mission in Texas at the time but Peter called me and told me of it. A tragic hit-and-run accident, wasn't it?''

"Yes. He was struck by a car three weeks ago when he walked outside his home to get his Sunday paper. At this time, Monterey detectives still have no leads or suspects on who might have been driving that car.''

He wasn't sure if Sophie actually made a tiny gasp or if he was simply attuned enough to her that he sensed her distress. Not that she gave much away. He thought her skin might have paled a shade or two but she looked as serene and composed as usual.

He turned back to the agents. "Do you suspect a connection between Walter Marlowe's death and the car accident that killed my brother and sister-in-law?''

The male agent spoke up. "It's too early in the investigation for us to comment on that.''

"Then why are you here?''

"While I can't give you any official comment,'' Herrera put in, "I can tell you that we are considering the possibility that the three deaths are related. The C.H.P. has asked us to assist them in the investigation of both incidents and so we are simply trying to follow all possible leads.''

"Are you implying none of the deaths was accidental?''

"That's certainly a possibility we're considering, Lieutenant."

He should never have insisted Sophie stay. He was keenly aware of each of her breaths—slow, measured, unnaturally even, as if she were practicing some deep metaphysical relaxation technique she'd probably learned in some ashram in India somewhere to stay in control.

Under other circumstances, he would have reached out and squeezed her fingers but he doubted she would welcome his comfort.

He couldn't blame her for her distress. It had been difficult enough to think of Peter and Shelly dying in a terrible accident, one so violent that Peter's body had been wrenched from the car and washed away.

He found the idea that their plunge into the Pacific might not have been so accidental completely horrifying.

He glanced at Sophie again and saw that the rhythm of her breathing had taken on a little hitch and her skin had paled another shade.

She shouldn't have to hear this kind of ugly speculation, not unless the FBI had something more concrete to go by than vague suspicion. He was tempted to ask her if she wanted to leave but he had a feeling she would refuse, no matter how difficult she might find staying here.

"Can you tell us why would you suspect the two incidents might be related?" he asked.

"So far, the Highway Patrol has been unable to determine any significant reason why your brother's Mercedes suddenly plunged over the Highway 1 guardrail. It's a complete mystery to the investigators."

"I was told it would be weeks before the C.H.P. would conclude its investigation."

"Yes, that's true. But they have done a preliminary investigation and could find no skid marks to indicate your brother might have swerved out of control and tried to overcorrect. Weather wasn't an issue since the roads were clear. Preliminary examination of the vehicle retrieved from the ocean doesn't indicate any evidence of mechanical failure. Peter Canfield had been drinking, according to witnesses at the party he and Mrs. Canfield attended in Big Sur, but in moderation. Without a body, we are of course unable to test for blood alcohol levels but alcohol is not believed to be a factor."

Sophie's hands were clenching and unclenching on her thighs, though he was fairly sure she was unaware of it. She looked as if she wanted to flee but she didn't move.

"Since no one who saw the accident has stepped forward," Herrera continued, "there is some speculation that perhaps another vehicle was involved. That someone else forced your brother off the road."

"Why share this information with us based on nothing but speculation?"

"We were actually hoping for some assistance. We hoped to ask your father if he might be aware of anyone with a grudge against the top brass at Canfield."

She let that sink in before continuing. "Since he is apparently unavailable, we'll ask you the same question. Do you know of any disgruntled employees, perhaps, or investors who might have lost a large amount of money and blamed the company?"

"I'm not involved in the day-to-day operations of Canfield. Not yet, anyway. But I can tell you that I do know the occasional unhappy customer is an unfortunate but inevitable part of investment banking."

"You never heard your father or brother mention anyone specifically?"

"No. I'm sorry."

"It would be most helpful to the investigation if we could speak with your father, Lieutenant."

Tom made a split-second decision. "My father suffers from moderate to severe Alzheimer's, Agent Herrera. He hasn't been directly involved with Canfield for the past three years."

Both agents looked surprised. "I'm sorry," Herrera said abruptly. "We were unaware of your father's condition."

"My brother chose to keep that information private."

"That does complicate things. Is there anyone else at Canfield who might have information about someone who would have a motive to harm top executives at the company?"

For once he wished he'd taken more of an interest in the business that had so obsessed his father and brother. "I don't know at this point but I'm meeting with the current Canfield executive board in the morning. I'll ask them if they have any information that might assist in the investigation."

"Thank you." Herrera rose and her junior partner followed suit. "Here's my card. We'll be in touch with you, then. And may we suggest that you take extra precautions for the next few weeks until we are able to proceed with the investigation. Perhaps you should advise the other executives at Canfield to do the same?"

"Do you really think more company officers might be at risk?"

"I don't want to unnecessarily alarm you. The two incidents—Walter Marlowe's hit-and-run death and the accident that killed your brother and sister-in-law—

might be entirely unrelated. But we don't like coincidences in the FBI. When the two chief officers of a company both die under questionable circumstances just a few weeks apart, it certainly warrants closer scrutiny."

"Of course. Thank you for stopping by."

"Are you okay?" Tom asked as soon as the door closed behind the federal agents.

Sophie tried to grab hold of her thoughts, which had been wildly scrambling for the past fifteen minutes. "No, I'm not. How could I be?" The control she had clung to so desperately started to slip away. "Someone might have deliberately run Peter and Shelly off the road!"

"As Herrera said, it's all speculation at this point. They don't really know anything, they're just fishing."

"But it could have been deliberate. Can you imagine anything more horrible?" She was cold, suddenly, chilled to the bone even though the radiant heating system in the house always maintained a constant seventy-two degrees. She crossed her arms to hold in her body heat but still couldn't control the slow shivers racking her body.

"Ever since you called me in Morocco, I've tried not to think about those last seconds before they…before they died. The horror and the fear and the awful helplessness as they went over that cliff. Now I can't think of anything else."

The distance she had worked so hard to pry out between her and Shelly's intertwined psyches seemed as thin and fragile now as old, brittle paper. Suddenly she could picture those last moments with terrible clarity, images so real and vivid she was sure it couldn't be strictly her imagination. It was almost as if she had been riding along in the back seat.

If she closed her eyes, she could hear muffled arguing then, oddly, a car door, then a strangled gasp in that weightless moment as Peter's sleek car hovered at the lip of the cliff before plummeting hundreds of feet to the waiting, relentless rocks below.

She heard a small cry and realized it was her own voice. She shook off the images and found Tom watching her, deep concern shadowing his silvery eyes.

"Oh, Tom. It must have been terrible. Shelly hated heights. Truly hated them."

"I know. I drove with her a few times to Big Sur and she was always a little nervous on Highway 1."

Had Shelly somehow had some subconscious premonition of her own death? Was that the reason she'd been edgy and upset at anything higher than a second-story window?

It was another of their dramatic differences. Sophie hadn't minded heights at all. She loved to shoot aerial views out of a single-engine plane and climb steep mountainsides in search of a new perspective.

"When we were kids, I used to be so mean and tease her about it. About disliking heights so much. I would climb the monkey bars at the park and tight-rope walk with no hands along the bars until Shelly, down on the ground, would be wringing her own hands and sobbing for me to get down. I would just laugh at her and call her a wimp."

Her voice broke with belated regret for the torment. "I loved my sister. Why would I do something so cruel?"

To her surprise, Tom pulled her into a somewhat awkward embrace, her head scrunched against the hard ridge of his shoulder. She didn't mind, too struck by an over-whelming sense of comfort, of rightness.

She'd needed this after the trauma of the FBI agents' visit, to be nestled against his strength and heat. Safe and protected and warm, even if only for a moment.

She sighed and edged closer, inhaling his scent, of expensive soap and clean laundry and Tom.

"You were a kid," he answered from somewhere above her head. "Kids can be real stinkers to each other."

Adults can be, too. She thought of the bewildering pain she had caused her sister these last ten years with her careful and deliberate defection. She would do any-thing to be able to go back and make a different choice, even though she didn't have the first idea what else she might have done.

The tears that seemed to have become her constant companion in the past few days burned behind her eye-lids, in her throat, and she fiercely tried to choke them back. She succeeded except for one small sob.

"Go ahead and cry if you need to," Thomas said gruffly above her head. "I won't melt."

It would be so tempting to give in. Just surrender to the press of emotions and weep in his arms.

She couldn't, though. She didn't dare. Already she could feel the seductive softening of her heart, feel all those old emotions she had fought so hard to bury fight-ing their way to the surface.

She didn't want them to re-emerge. She didn't know if she could bear it.

He would never know the effort it took her to choke down those emotions and step away from his comfort. "I'd better go check to make sure the children aren't running Mrs. Cope ragged."

He wore a strange expression and opened his mouth as if to say something but then apparently changed his mind and stepped even farther away.

"Yes. That's probably a good idea."

She turned toward the door but his voice stopped her. "Sophie, thank you for staying. It helped to have you here. But if I'd known what they were here about, I never would have asked you to stay. I'm sorry I put you through that."

She gazed at him, looking strong and masculine and gorgeous in the waning light spilling through the window. Oh, it would be far too easy to fall for him all over again.

She drew in a deep breath, searching for that damn elusive center of control inside herself. With a nod, she turned and left the room to find the children.

Chapter 7

A few hours later Sophie sat on the edge of Peter and Shelly's bed combing wet tangles out of Ali's long hair. Thomas was reading with the twins in their bedroom and the house was quiet, settled.

She had to admit, these bedtime rituals were starting to grow on her. She loved these quiet moments with Ali when the two of them could talk without the constant chatter of the twins.

At ten, Ali showed remarkable depths, Sophie was discovering. Conversing with her was a joy—her niece had a quick, lively mind and Shelly's quiet sense of humor.

As much as she enjoyed listening to Ali's conversation, Sophie had to admit after the stress of the day, she found this hairbrushing routine soothing. It was something she and Shelly used to do for each other, so sharing it with Shelly's daughter was like walking down a comfortable, familiar pathway.

The brush caught on a particularly snarled section and Ali winced.

"Sorry. I didn't mean to yank."

"It's okay. It didn't hurt much," her niece replied.

"Well, I'm almost finished."

"Okay." Ali paused, then without turning her head she shifted her gaze to meet Sophie's. "Aunt Sophie, did those people who were here earlier want to talk to you and Uncle Tommy about my mom and dad?"

The sudden question took her off guard and for several moments Sophie scrambled for what to say. She couldn't very well tell the child what the FBI agents had said, about the possibility that someone might have deliberately caused the crash that killed Peter and Shelly. Not when, as Tom pointed out, they had little more on which to base suspicion at this point than a handful of speculation.

On the other hand, she didn't want to lie to the girl, either. She and Shelly had been fed a steady diet of lies and half truths by Sharon. Sometimes she didn't think her mother really knew the difference between the truth and a convenient lie.

What used to really baffle her was that Sharon chose stupid things to lie about, too, like whether the power bill had been paid and why her new boyfriend wore a hairpiece.

Sharon hadn't cared whether her lies were at all believable or not. Even two seven-year-old girls weren't naive enough to really think their father had been a famous country-music star who would have married Sharon except he already had a wife and family.

Even then, as young as they had been, they accepted that Sharon probably hadn't had a clue who their father was. They did know it was unlikely he had been a famous country-music star or Sharon would have figured out a way to milk the man for everything he had.

As a result of growing up in Sharon's fantasy world, Sophie had vowed if she ever had children, she would try her best to be straight with them whenever possible.

"Yes," she finally answered Ali. "They're part of the investigation into what caused the crash."

That was truthful, as far as it went. It just wasn't the whole truth.

"Do they…do they know anything yet?"

"No. Not yet, sweetheart."

She prayed Ali would let the topic drop. To her relief, her niece didn't seem any more eager to probe the painful topic than Sophie.

"Mama always brushed my hair before I went to bed," Ali said after a moment. "It always helped me fall right to sleep."

Her heart ached with sympathy for all Ali had lost. She set aside the brush and gave her a quick hug. "Your mom and I used to brush each other's hair when we were your age. You're right, I always found it very relaxing. There were lots of times when I was traveling when I would have been willing to give away every single thing in my suitcase just to have someone sit with me and brush my hair before bedtime."

"I'm going to miss it," Ali said in a quiet little whisper that just about shattered Sophie's heart into a million pieces.

The twins' occasional flashes of baffled grief were certainly not easy to deal with. But Sophie wondered if in many ways Ali wouldn't feel the loss of her parents more keenly.

She was at an age where she and Shelly had been starting to lay the groundwork for a deeper, more mature relationship. In her infrequent visits, Sophie had seen enough of the bond between her sister and Ali to know the girl had lost not only her mother but her friend.

More than anything, she wished she had words that might give comfort but she knew nothing would ease this pain. Time might take away some of the brutal sting but the emptiness would always be there.

"Oh, honey," she finally murmured. "I'll keep brushing your hair every night just as long as you want me to. That's a solemn vow."

Ali looked over her shoulder and offered up a tiny smile. Sophie fought the urge to pull the child into her arms again and engage in another good cry. That would do nothing but upset Ali, though. Besides, she had done enough weeping for one night. Enough for a lifetime of nights.

She managed a smile in return then looked away quickly before Ali could be upset further by the tears she feared were gathering in her eyes. Her gaze landed on the mantel of the ornate white marble fireplace in the room. A flash of shiny red sparkled against the pale marble like rubies spilled in snow.

"Oh!" she exclaimed, setting down the brush and walking to the mantel for a closer look. "Will you look at this? This is the lacquer box I sent your mother from one of my first overseas assignments! It was from this tiny fishing village on the Black Sea in Russia. I was wandering through the market and spied this little old lady sitting in front of a whole stall overflowing with these. She was the sweetest lady. I couldn't resist her or her boxes, especially when I saw this one. I can't believe Shelly kept it all this time!"

Ali joined her. "Mama loved that box. She always said that whenever she looked at it, you didn't seem so far away. She could almost pretend she was seeing the world right along with you.''

That damn relentless guilt pinched at her again. ''I bought it because the angel painted on it reminded me of your mother. See, she has the same pretty blond hair and green eyes?''

''That's funny. She always said it reminded her of you.''

Sophie wrinkled up her nose. ''I don't think so. I'm not very angelic-looking, am I?''

Ali laughed, as Sophie had hoped she would. ''She does look more like my mama than you.''

On impulse, she took the box from the shelf and held it out to her niece. ''Al, why don't you take it?''

Ali gasped. ''Can I?''

If she were to get technical, Sophie supposed the box could be considered part of Shelly's estate, something to be disposed of by the executor. But it was only an inexpensive souvenir box with little value beyond sentiment. Since it had been her own gift to her sister, she didn't think Tom would mind if she gave it now to Ali.

''It's yours. Put it somewhere in your room, and then whenever you see it you can remember that an angel who looks just like that one watches over you and the twins now.''

Ali's radiant smile glowed brighter than a fire under that mantel ever could. She was so pleased that Sophie only wished she could find that little grandmother in Jurilovca and buy two more exactly like it for the twins. She would have to find something else of Shelly's to give them.

''Come on. Let's find a spot of honor for it in your bedroom.''

After considering all her options, Ali finally settled on her bedside table as a new home for the box.

"That way, I can see it every night before I fall asleep."

"Good idea." Sophie touched her shoulder, then the two of them went in search of the twins for a last goodnight.

When they walked through the door of the twins' room, Sophie opened her mouth to apologize for taking so long with Ali's hair, then stopped short, struck by the sight that greeted them.

The twins were sharing Zoe's bed, curly heads close together as they bent over a picture book, while their uncle was stretched out on the other bed, his shoes off. He was fast asleep, a book whose title she couldn't see open on his chest.

Sophie had so rarely seen him in such a vulnerable state that she could do nothing but stare at the picture he made. He looked so much younger in sleep, relaxed, without the commanding authority usually stamped on his strong features.

He was gorgeous enough when he was awake. At rest like this, she found him devastating. She wanted to smooth that lock of dark hair away from his face, to tuck a quilt around his shoulders, to lie beside him and feel his chest rise and fall with the rhythm of each breath....

"Shhh," Zoe whispered. "Uncle Tommy fell asleep."

"I can see that," Sophie whispered back, reining in her inappropriate thoughts. "Did you get a story first?"

"He started to read us one but didn't get very far so we decided to read to ourselves," Zach answered.

Sophie smiled. "That was nice of you to let your uncle get some rest. He's working really hard right now."

"Just like Daddy always did," Zoe said with a little grimace. "That's why Mommy said he didn't have time to play with us very much, 'cause he always had to work."

She wondered if Peter would have made more opportunities to spend with his children if he knew his time with them would be cut so brutally short. Probably not. She doubted anything would be able to change her opinion that the man had been a total bastard who didn't give a single damn about his children.

"Why don't we all go have one more story in the other room so Uncle Tommy can rest a little longer."

They agreed and slipped down from Zoe's bed. The three children followed her back into the room she had taken as her own by default, Peter and Shelly's room.

Though she still felt a little strange staying here, it made the most sense that she continue using it. This was the only available bedroom in this part of the house. If she wanted to be close to the children, this was just about her only option.

Tom had a room downstairs, closer to his father's apartment. If she slept downstairs in one of the guest rooms in the other wing of the house, there would be no one nearby if one of the twins woke and needed something in the night.

The children seemed to find comfort being here, anyway. By their easy familiarity with the room, she had a feeling they had spent a great deal of time with Shelly here.

They read one short story. Though all three children begged for another, Sophie tried to be firm. "Come on. You all have school tomorrow. You need your rest."

"We haven't said our prayers, Aunt Sophie," Zoe said suddenly on the way out the door.

"We haven't said them in a while," Zach added.

"We probably should," Ali offered.

Right. Prayers. Every time she turned around, Sophie stumbled into another area of parenthood she should be remembering.

She hoped they knew what they were doing in the prayer department because it wasn't exactly her area of expertise.

She could tell them about Santeria and Taoism and Umbanda. But when it came to any kind of organized Western religion, her experience was limited to a brief summer when Sharon had sent her and Shelly to a free Bible school run by a local Pentecostal congregation.

Sophie suspected her mother's motives had more to do with getting the girls out of her hair for a couple hours during the day than out of any compelling desire to have them find God. She remembered snippets of a few rousing songs and making bottle art out of layers of colored sand but that was about it.

She made a mental note to ask Tom if he knew what church Shelly and Peter had attended with the children so she could make an effort to take them. That was exactly the kind of continuity that would help them cope with the loss of their parents.

To her relief, the children didn't appear to need much help from her with their prayers. They knelt by the side of the bed and each took turns murmuring a few phrases.

Zoe made her smile when she asked for new rollerblades so she could skate exactly like her sister and her poor battered heart cracked a little more when each child prayed that their parents would be happy in Heaven.

After the last amen, she stood up. "Time for bed now, piglets. Come on, no more excuses."

"Aunt Sophie, where should I sleep tonight?" Zach asked. "Uncle Tommy is in my bed."

"Not anymore," a deep voice spoke from the doorway.

All of them looked quickly toward the door. Tom stood with his shoulder propped against the jamb, his hair slightly mussed and sleepy shadows lingering in his eyes. Her breathing kicked up a notch and she wondered how long he'd been standing there watching them.

"See. Problem solved," she said to Zach, hoping nobody else noticed the little hitch in her voice. "Now scoot, you guys."

She delivered hugs and kisses then watched as the children received more of the same from their uncle. After the last hug, they finally headed for their respective bedrooms, leaving her and Tom alone.

All this domesticity never failed to unnerve her. Of all the men she'd ever met, Thomas Canfield was the last one she might have expected to find herself running a family with.

She wasn't sure exactly why, but she couldn't help thinking it was oddly disturbing that they seemed to work so well together, at least when it came to the children.

Maybe because the rest of the time—when it was just the two of them, like now—a subtle tension hummed and sparked between them.

His mouth twisted ruefully. "I guess I didn't do a very good job with storytime. Sorry about that."

"I didn't mind reading to them. I like it, actually. Besides, you looked as if you could use the rest."

"It has been a hairy couple of days. I have a feeling things will only get worse from this point, especially if there are problems at Canfield I don't know about."

His words served as a grim reminder of their meeting with the FBI agents earlier. All evening she'd been trying not to dwell on the terrible possibility that Shelly and Peter might have been murdered.

"Tom, will you keep me informed?" she asked suddenly. "I would like to know if you find anything that might lead you to believe Shelly and Peter's accident was caused by someone else."

He looked surprised at her request. "Of course I will. Do you really think I would try to keep something like that from you?"

She shrugged. "Both of us know any problems at Canfield are really none of my business. It's your family's firm and I'm really not family."

"I meant what I said to the FBI. You have as much right to know what happened on that highway as I do. You're part of this."

She smiled a little to convey her gratitude, then her breath caught when his gaze shifted to her mouth. Something wild and hot kindled in his eyes.

He wanted to kiss her. She'd never been more sure of anything in her life. Her stomach fluttered and started a long, slow burn.

They stood looking at each other for a long moment while the air around them seemed to sizzle and pop, then Tom finally wrenched his gaze away.

"I'd better get back to work. Good night."

With a jerky abruptness at odds with his usual athletic grace, he turned and walked from the room.

For a long time, Sophie stood by the bed staring at an empty doorway while her pulse raced and her insides quivered like the time she'd been caught in an earthquake in Colombia.

* * *

This was getting to be a bad habit.

Sophie glanced at the glowing LCD numbers of the clock by her bed. A little after 1:00 a.m. and something had awakened her again. She sighed and stretched a kink out of her neck. This was probably the most luxurious mattress she'd slept on in months, yet she hadn't had a full night's sleep since she got here.

She tried to put a finger on what had awakened her but couldn't come up with anything concrete, just a vague feeling that something wasn't as it should be.

Perhaps one of the children had awakened. The room was dim, lit only by weak moonlight filtering in through the windows, but she glanced toward the door that led into the hallway.

Hadn't she left it ajar for this very reason, so she could hear the children if one of them cried out in the night?

She frowned and switched on the low-watt lamp by the bed. As soon as she did, she realized what must have happened. After her encounter with Tom she'd been restless and unable to sleep. She remembered opening the sliding door leading to the balcony so she could enjoy the cool, sweetly scented night air coming in off the garden.

She must have fallen asleep before she had a chance to close it again. A strong breeze easily could have blown through and closed the door. That might even have been what awakened her.

She rose from the bed and grabbed the silky emerald robe she'd bought off a street vendor in Bali, then opened the door into the hallway first, listening to make sure none of the children were stirring. Satisfied after several moments that they were still sleeping, she crossed the room to the sliding doors.

Instead of closing them as she had intended, she

paused, struck by the view. Through the spindly tree trunks she could see moonlight gleaming on the water. Wispy tendrils of fog drifted off the sea, curving sinuously through the trees.

She loved it here as much as her sister had, this spectacular meeting of land and sea. It was the ancient call of the ocean, she supposed, as seductive and powerful as a lover's kiss.

She loved the view and she loved the smells and she loved the low, constant murmur of the ocean.

On impulse, she slid open the doors and walked out onto the balcony, shivering a little at the cool tiles beneath her bare feet. She settled into a thick, cushioned chair Shelly had probably set out for exactly this purpose and drew her feet under her, enjoying the night and another psychic link to her sister.

She hadn't been out long when she heard it, something that didn't quite seem to fit the peaceful night—the quiet finality of a door clicking open and closed somewhere below her.

She scanned the shadows below her. She couldn't see anything unusual at first. Then she gasped as a darker shadow moved out across the moonlit grass and disappeared into the fog-shrouded trees.

William!

Chapter 8

Her first instinct was to run down the steps and chase after him but William was moving quickly, hurrying as if he had a purpose in mind, unlike the night of the funeral when she had found him standing disoriented and helpless at the top of the redwood steps.

She would never be able to find him in the darkness and fog without a flashlight and in thick woods she was unfamiliar with.

This time, he didn't seem to be heading toward the beach but had gone into the trees that divided Seal Point from a neighboring estate.

She needed to notify Thomas. He knew the area and might have some idea where his father might be heading in his altered mental state. Aware with every passing second that the potential for disaster loomed ever greater, she rushed down the stairs and ran down the hall to Thomas's room, then knocked urgently on the door.

"Tom? Thomas? Are you there?"

After a long moment when she began to fear perhaps he might still be working in his office at the other end of the house, a sleep-roughened voice answered.

"Yeah."

Under the door she saw a sliver of light appear as he must have turned on a lamp. "Come in. What's wrong?"

She opened the door. "I think your father's left the house again," she said quickly.

His oath was low and heartfelt and he thrust aside the blankets covering him. He jumped from the bed so quickly Sophie didn't even have time to look away when she realized he wore a pair of navy blue boxer shorts and nothing else.

He yanked on jeans then shoved his feet into a pair of boots by the bed and headed for the door. "How do you know he left?" he asked without waiting to see if she followed him.

She hurried after him, aware of the complete inappropriateness given the gravity of the situation, of noticing the way the firm muscles of his bare shoulders rippled down to a narrow waist.

She cleared her throat and focused on the crisis at hand. "Something woke me. I walked outside on the balcony for a little fresh air and saw someone leave the house, heading for the trees. I couldn't see anything but a dark shape, really, but I knew it must be your father. I would have gone after him but I didn't have a flashlight in my room. Since I feared I would only get lost if I went to look for him myself, I thought it would be best to let you know."

By now they had reached William's apartment, which consisted of a small sitting room with a door leading outside, an efficiency kitchen and two bedrooms, one for him and one for the nurse.

Tom flipped on a light in the sitting room and moved quickly to his father's bedroom door. When he opened it, Sophie couldn't see around his broad frame but she heard his audible sigh of relief, then the rustle of bedcovers from inside.

"Peter?" William's voice sounded sleepy and disoriented. "Is that you, Peter? What are you doing out of bed at this hour?"

Relief soaked through her. William was safe and sound in his bed.

But if he hadn't been wandering around outside at 2:00 a.m., who else could it have been?

"No. It's me, Dad. Tom. I was just checking on you."

"Tom, tell your brother to stop his nonsense and go to sleep. You've both got school tomorrow."

Thomas was silent for a moment, then he nodded. "Sure, Dad. I'll tell him. Good night."

He closed the door softly and was reaching to turn off the light when the door to the other bedroom in the apartment opened and the nurse, Maura, walked out wearing a ruffled flannel robe that would have done a Victorian maiden proud.

"Is everything all right? What's going on?"

"We just had a scare, Maura," Tom said. "We were afraid Dad might have gone wandering off again."

"I'd like to see the man try. He would have to have some kind of magic wand to get out without setting off all those bells and alarms you hung on the outside door. If he tries to leave again, I guarantee I'll hear the racket. If I don't, we can both go down to the drug store together so I can buy myself the loudest hearing aids I can find."

Tom smiled. "Well, at any rate, there's been a mistake. He's tucked in bed, right where he should be."

"I'm sorry we disturbed you, Mrs. McMurray," Sophie said.

"Don't worry a thing about it. I'm sure I'll fall right back asleep in two shakes. I'm just glad he didn't go haring off again."

Tom bid the nurse good-night, then he led the way back into the hall outside his father's apartment.

"I saw someone leaving the house, Tom. I know I did," Sophie said after the door closed behind them.

He couldn't doubt her sincerity, not with the worry still shading her eyes. "It's a dark night with little moonlight. The ocean fog can play tricks on the eyes."

"It wasn't a trick of the fog or a figment of my imagination. I saw someone."

He sighed. He didn't want to hurt her feelings by actively doubting her story but he couldn't agree.

"I believe you *think* you saw someone. But it's impossible. Who could it have been? Anybody trying to get in or out of the house would trip the alarms unless he knew the code, which no one outside the immediate family has. Beyond that, there are motion-sensors around the grounds and someone would have to know where every single one is to make it through without raising a hell of a ruckus."

She stuck out that determined little chin of hers. "I'm not crazy. I saw someone."

"I don't believe you're crazy."

"But you think I'm seeing things."

"I've had similar experiences out there in the fog. Once when I was on a night mission I could swear I saw an entire fleet of schooners floating below us. Turned out to be only fog, not a ghost ship."

"It wasn't fog or a ghost. I don't like this at all, Tom. Not after what Herrera and Washburn had to say today. What if this is somehow linked to the crash?"

He held out a hand. "Let's not jump ahead of ourselves. In the morning I'll contact the company that handles security at Seal Point to see if they noted anything unusual on the computers during the night. We'll go from there, okay?"

She nodded and for the first time since she came to his room, he noticed what she was wearing—a robe of rich emerald that perfectly matched her eyes.

It looked silky and exotic and made him think of warm island breezes and sun-bronzed skin. He couldn't help wondering what it would feel like sliding through his fingers.

Probably as soft as that wild froth of hair curling loose over her shoulders.

He shouldn't allow himself to wonder such things. They would only end up torturing him through a sleepless night he could ill afford.

Still, the low light in the hallway lent a seductive intimacy to the moment. It would be so easy to pull her close, to bury his hands in that silky robe and lose himself in the heat of her mouth.

He jerked his mind away from that dangerous path. "What were you doing up at this hour anyway?"

Her mouth twisted into a rueful smile. "To be honest, I'm not quite sure. Something woke me and I realized I had fallen asleep with the sliding door to the balcony open. I went to close it and was drawn out by the stillness of the night. I was out there for only a few moments watching the moonlight on the water when I saw your father leaving the house. Or what I thought was your father."

"Even though it wasn't Dad, I appreciate your concern. For some reason I've always had the impression the two of you didn't care much for each other, back before his condition developed."

She opened her mouth to answer him, then Tom had the distinct impression she changed her mind about whatever she had been planning to say.

"I barely knew your father," she murmured instead, her attention fixed on a small glass sculpture gracing a table in the hallway. "I don't know why you would possibly think William and I had anything other than a polite relationship."

He tried to think what might have given him that idea but couldn't put a finger on any one specific thing. It was more like a vague impression. An instinct. A look of subtle distaste in his father's eyes, maybe, when Shelly would talk about her twin or something Peter might have said.

He tried to remember the dynamics between Sophie and William the few times he'd seen them together, those two weeks a decade ago and then when the twins were born and Sophie had stopped for a quick visit between assignments.

No, he was sure of it. He was positive he had detected a certain coolness lingering between the two of them. But since she didn't seem inclined to enlighten him as to the reason—and his father couldn't—he decided to let the matter drop.

"I must be mistaken, then."

He was about to bid good-night when she changed the subject.

"The children will be going back to school tomorrow."

"You don't think it's too soon?"

"I told you I'm no expert on this whole parenting thing but my gut instinct tells me they need to return to some kind of regular routine as quickly as possible. I have to think that returning to school—keeping busy with schoolwork and their friends—will help keep their minds off the deaths of their parents as much as possible."

"Don't sell those gut instincts short," he answered. "So far I think they've been right on the money when it comes to knowing what's best for Ali and the twins."

She raised one delicate eyebrow. "And here I was under the impression you thought I was a bad influence on them. Something to do with my not having one smidgeon of anything resembling common sense, I believe you said."

"You're not going to forget that, are you?"

She laughed. "Probably not. You were right, of course. I don't have much common sense."

It was becoming increasingly difficult for him to reconcile this soft, pleasing woman with the selfish, irresponsible Sophie who came and went as she pleased without any regard to the feelings of anyone she might be leaving behind.

"I shouldn't have said that. Again, I apologize. I was upset and worried about them. I must admit, they don't seem to have suffered any lasting damage from their rainy-day swim."

He paused, fighting down the urge to twist one of those errant curls around his finger and tug her close. "I'm trying to tell you I think you're doing a good job with them."

"I love them, Thomas. No matter what else you might think of me, please don't doubt that."

"I don't."

Still, he couldn't help wondering and worrying if love would be enough to keep her here.

"I'm glad you're here. I would have been in a real mess without you, especially with these latest developments. I don't know how I would have been able to give the children the attention they need—the attention they deserve—while trying to handle everything at Canfield and my father, too. You've been good for them, Sophie."

She gazed at him out of those huge green eyes and he was surprised to see what might have been the sheen of tears glimmering in the dimly lit hallway. "Thank you," she murmured.

They fell into a not-uncomfortable silence as the big house shifted and settled around them. He knew he should let her return to bed—they would both need all the rest they could find to help them face the challenges of the coming day.

He knew how much energy it took to keep up with Ali and the twins. And in the morning he would have to try to make his way in a world he had shunned a long time ago.

He should walk her back to her bedroom but he was loathe to leave her, reluctant to abandon this tiny oasis of peace in a life that seemed suddenly to be adrift through one turbulent storm after another.

"Sophie."

She turned toward him as he said her name. If he hadn't caught that glimpse of awareness in her eyes, he might have said good-night and left her before he did something stupid.

But he *did* see it, glittering there like the beacon on the Point Piños lighthouse, a mirror image of his own desire.

With a resigned sigh, he stepped forward and kissed her.

At the first touch of his mouth she froze, her body stiff and unwieldy in his arms, and he had the terrible feeling he had just committed a grievous error in judgment, crossed some invisible but vitally necessary barrier between them.

He started to pull away but before he could, her mouth softened and she whispered out a sigh that vibrated down his spine as her hands crept up to rest tentatively on his bare chest.

At her response, a whole host of answering emotions swamped him. He deepened the kiss, pulling her closer. She was tall, willowy, and fit against him with the same sweet perfection he remembered from a decade ago, as if she had never left his arms.

It had been so long since he'd held her but somehow he remembered exactly how she would feel in his arms, how she would taste. Kissing her was exactly as he remembered, the same wild rush of heat and stunning sorcery and an overwhelming sense of *rightness*, that he belonged exactly here.

Her mouth was warm and tasted of citrus and mint and he wanted to devour every inch of her, from those sexy tousled curls to the pink-painted toenails peeking out from her robe.

For the moment he contented himself with her mouth and kissed her with all the pent-up passion he hadn't realized he'd been hoarding only for her.

The silk of her robe brushed against his bare chest with every breath, tantalizing his nerve endings to a fever pitch. What had seemed so alluring earlier was now painfully erotic against his skin.

He dragged his mouth away from hers and trailed soft

kisses down her neck, then pushed aside her robe. She wore a plain sleeveless nightgown underneath and somehow he found that every bit as alluring as that sensuous robe.

Her head lolled back, bumping gently against the wall, and he pushed aside the strap of her nightgown to kiss the soft, warm skin at the apex where shoulder met neck.

"You smell just as I remember. Exotic and wild and delicious."

A muscle in her neck trembled against his lips and he left the enticing expanse of skin to return to her mouth. She kissed him with such eagerness that he had to ask the question burning through him like a forest fire consuming dry tinder.

"Why did you leave so abruptly ten years ago, Sophie? It seemed to me one moment you were in my arms just like this, and the next you were catching the next flight out of town."

How did he expect her to carry on a conversation when all she could focus on was the wonder of being in his arms again?

She tried to catch hold of her thoughts that his kiss had scattered like seed pods on a stiff wind, but she had little success. "Bus," she managed, her insides weak and trembling. "I took a Greyhound. I couldn't afford a flight then."

"Whatever," he growled. "It doesn't matter how you left, I guess. Just that you did."

Somehow his words made a jagged tear in the glorious haze of desire and comfort that surrounded her like a warm quilt on a cold night. She blinked back to awareness and realized he had stepped away slightly, just enough to allow cool air to slide between them.

"Was I the only one who thought we were poised on the brink of something real? Something right?" he asked, his voice low, intense. "Before we had a chance to even explore what that might be, you ran away without a word."

She shivered and drew in a shuddering breath, trying fiercely to regain her equilibrium. He wanted to know why she left and she couldn't begin to find the words to tell him.

"I left you a note. I explained it."

"A few scribbled words that didn't explain squat."

"I told you I had a…a job waiting for me. I'd been away long enough."

"You were scared so you ran away."

She couldn't deny his words, not when the truth of them resonated through her like the clear, deep toll of the bells of La Giralda cathedral she had heard in Seville a few months earlier.

She *had* been scared. Young and terrified and hopelessly out of her league.

But she hadn't been scared of Tom.

Never of him.

Still, she knew she couldn't tell him what he wanted to know. "I should return to my room," she murmured and was relieved when her voice came out cool and steady. "The children have school early."

"You're doing it again. Running away."

"From what? It was only a kiss. A brief encounter between two people in a darkened hallway in the middle of the night."

"You can fool yourself into thinking that's all it is if you want. But we both know better."

She didn't want to face this. Not now. ''Good night, Thomas. I'm sorry I woke you for nothing.''

She yanked her robe back over her shoulder and hurried for the stairs and the safety of her room.

Chapter 9

Back in her room, Sophie drew a deep breath and tried to block the memories whipping through her mind hard and fast.

It was as useless as trying to hold back the sea. She pressed a hand to her still-fluttering stomach, then wandered to the window.

Sleep would be a long time coming, she feared, if it was even possible at all tonight. Too many doubts and regrets and memories tangled through her for her to be able to find rest.

With a resigned sigh, she picked up a colorful quilt off the chest at the foot of the bed and opened the sliding doors to the outside. The cool night air caressed her with the sweet fragrance of fall-blooming flowers and the tang of the ocean as she returned to the cushioned chair she had left only a short time ago.

Knowing the wild rush of memories would take over whether she wanted them there or not, she tucked her legs under her and watched the moonlight glimmer on the distant waves and let herself remember.

She had nearly been twenty-one that summer. A child, barely even a woman.

Though she hadn't really been so young, she supposed. Shelly had been the same age and she was already a wife and a mother, deliriously happy at the fulfillment of all her dreams.

Sophie hated to admit it, but her sister's new life had left her feeling adrift, disconnected to the one person who had always been her anchor, her best friend.

Her other half.

She had been so lonely after Shelly's marriage, more lonely than she'd ever been in her life. She wanted her sister to be happy but she couldn't help wondering what would happen to her without Shelly.

Maybe that's why her heart had been so vulnerable to Tom, because she had been looking for something to fill the void left by her sister's new life.

No, she thought. Even if she had met Tom under completely different circumstances, she knew she still would have been just as drawn to him. He was everything she admired in a man, strong and smart and fiercely independent.

The first few days at Seal Point—before Tom entered the picture—she had been restless and eager to leave this grand estate by the sea. She didn't belong here. Neither of them did. How could the illegitimate daughters of a rambling cocktail waitress like Sharon hope to belong in a world of old money and prestige like Seal Point?

Barbara Canfield—William's wife—had tried for Shelly's sake to be polite to her daughter-in-law's profligate twin sister. But Sophie hadn't been fooled. She had seen the disappointment on Barbara's perfectly made-up features whenever she looked at her youngest son's bride.

The Canfields were not happy about the marriage. Sophie had the strong impression Peter's parents would have preferred things if Shelly had taken her unplanned pregnancy and disappeared back into the trailer-trash world she came from.

Shelly seemed oblivious to it all, too wrapped up in her husband and her beautiful baby daughter, but Sophie had sensed it and resented like hell any inference that her sister might not be worthy to bear the great and exalted name of Canfield.

After only a few days, she had been itchy to leave the oppressive atmosphere at the estate, to return to New York and her photo internship at *Traveler* magazine and the tiny fourth-floor walkup in the Village she shared with three other girls.

The only thing holding her at Seal Point had been her promise to Shelly to stay at least until Ali's christening, a week away.

And then Thomas had arrived, home on a brief leave from his Coast Guard assignment in Alaska.

She vividly remembered her first glimpse of him. She had been in the elaborately decorated nursery one rainy afternoon rocking Ali and crooning softly to the fussy infant in the hopes that she might be able to let Shelly catch a little more badly needed sleep.

The child seemed finally ready to drift back to sleep herself. The room was warm and dim and she found an unexpected contentment softly rocking a tiny baby girl.

Sophie closed her eyes for just a moment, lulled by the peace of the moment, when she gradually became aware that the door had opened and a stranger stood in the doorway.

He was gorgeous, with dark hair cut military-short, silvery-blue eyes and chiseled, tanned features. On a purely abstract, professional level, she would have loved to photograph him, somewhere rugged and wild like a granite mountaintop somewhere with the wind ruffling that hair and his face turned to the sun.

On a far more intensely personal level, she just wanted to sit there and stare.

Before she could say anything, he walked toward her. Without speaking, he looked down at the baby for a moment then lifted his head and kissed Sophie on the cheek. He smelled divine, she remembered, that elusive masculine scent, and for one insane moment she wanted to turn her face into his skin and just inhale.

"She's beautiful," he murmured. "I should have known any daughter of yours would be a real stunner."

This must be Peter's brother, she realized. Her first thought was that he must have mistaken her for Shelly. Her second: that her sister had to be nuts to fall for a weasel like Peter with his far more attractive brother around. "Um, thanks. But she's not mine. I'm Sophie, Shelly's sister. Don't worry, people get us mixed up all the time."

He blinked and she thought she saw a hint of color tinge his cheeks in the dim room. "Sorry. My mistake. I'm Tom Canfield. Peter's older brother."

"Right. The chopper pilot."

"Yeah."

"Welcome home."

He looked vaguely surprised at her words, as if he didn't expect them from anyone here. "Thanks. So where is Shelly?"

"Napping. This little rascal isn't sleeping very well at night. I was trying to see if I could let her squeeze out ten more minutes before we go in to wake up the chow wagon.'' She paused and studied him. ''Would you like to hold our niece?''

''Me?''

''Sure. Nothing to it. Here, sit down.'' She rose from the rocking chair and gestured for him to sit. After a wary moment, he complied and she gingerly handed over the baby.

To her amusement, he held Ali with awkward care, as if she were a live grenade and someone had just yanked out the pin. After a moment, though, he began to relax a little and even reached a finger out to stroke the soft skin of the baby's cheek. Sophie wasn't quite sure why the sight of those strong fingers showing such tenderness to a tiny baby sent her insides whirling and twirling.

She cleared her throat. ''See? Nothing to it.''

He grinned at her, then his smile softened as he looked down at the tiny baby in his arms and Sophie had to fight hard to keep from melting all over the carpet in a boneless heap.

Instead, she leaned against the crib and watched him croon to their shared niece for a few moments until Ali started to fret.

He gazed at Sophie with a slightly helpless look. ''What am I supposed to do now?''

''This is where we find Shelly and make our escape,'' she said with a laugh.

Over the next few days, she and Tom spent a great deal of time escaping together. Shelly, wrapped up with Ali, really didn't need Sophie's help, so Tom offered to take her sightseeing around the Monterey Peninsula.

She had a feeling he volunteered to show her around, at least at first, more as an excuse to get away from what she quickly deduced was a complicated situation at Seal Point than out of any compelling desire to spend time with her.

He and his father had obvious differences of opinion about many things, not the least of which was Tom's military career, and whenever they were together tension hovered between them, heavy and taut with unspoken arguments.

While she felt vaguely guilty for taking Tom away from his family during the brief time he could visit, she had to admit she found his company intoxicating. He challenged her mind and thrilled her senses and made her laugh.

Together they shopped at all the funky little shops in Carmel and took a whale-watching cruise, where she was embarrassingly seasick and watched the sunset off Asilomar.

He kissed her for the first time three days after he arrived home. One night at dinner with the family, Sophie announced her intention to rise early and drive down the coast to photograph the Point Sur lighthouse in the sweet light at sunrise.

Tom volunteered to take her, as she had secretly hoped he would. Early in the morning, they sneaked out of the house, laughing and whispering together like children.

After the curving drive down the coast, Thomas pulled his Jeep into a narrow overlook off the highway where he assured her she would be able to get spectacular shots as soon as the sun started to rise.

They leaned against his Jeep sipping hot coffee from a thermos and nibbling on a couple of Mrs. Cope's divine cinnamon rolls they'd stolen out of the Seal Point kitchen, and watched the light change from black to lavender to pearl.

When the sun finally burst above the mountains—revealing a vast, stunning expanse of cliff and ocean and sky and the slim lighthouse perched on its own steep island—she had been breathless with the sheer raw beauty of it all.

She hadn't been able to squeeze off more than a few frames when without warning, he reached for her and kissed her. His warm mouth tasted of cinnamon sugar and coffee and just like that, her foolish heart had tumbled into love like a pebble tossed into the sea.

Over the next week before Ali's christening, Thomas took every opportunity to kiss her as often as possible. They kissed in the moonlit gardens at Seal Point, in a stand of towering redwoods off Highway 1, over clam chowder on Cannery Row.

They didn't talk about the future, about the unalterable fact that they lived thousands of miles apart, that they might not see each other again.

Sophie wouldn't let herself think about all those things. For the first time in her life she didn't focus on her carefully laid plans for the future, a future she would build herself. Instead, she lived only in the moment, only for the thrill of being with Tom and that painful flush of first love.

Finally, the night before Ali's christening—the night before she was to leave to return to her job in New York—they had wandered hand in hand down the long redwood stairway down the cliff to the beach.

He carried a blanket over his arm and a bottle of wine and anticipation thrummed through her.

This was it.

The entire week had been building inexorably toward

this moment. The evening breeze was warm, pleasant, but she barely noticed it, too consumed with the man she had fallen for so hard.

The small, secluded beach was private, accessible only by the Seal Point stairway. When they reached the sand, Thomas spread the blanket just above tide level then settled her onto it. They sat together gazing at the sunset, not saying much, just savoring this last time together.

Right before the sun slipped beneath the sea, he turned to her and kissed her passionately.

"I want to make love to you."

She shivered at the rough note of desire vibrating through his voice. Answering heat trembled through her. "What's stopping you?" she murmured, trying hard to sound sophisticated, as if she had done this dozens of times before.

"I don't want you thinking I bring hundreds of women down here. What we have had this week has been incredible."

He paused and in the last dying rays of the sun, his features looked as if they had been hewn from the same rock as the cliffs towering above them. "I care about you, Sophie. I wasn't looking for it. Heaven knows, I'm still not sure I'm ready for it, but you just knocked me on my butt from the first time I heard you laugh."

She laughed. "Oh, that's very flattering. I don't think I've ever knocked anyone on his, um, rear end before."

This was an amazing night, she thought as he laughed along with her and kissed her again. It was the most magical, intense night of her life and she wanted to remember every bit of it, from the murmuring sea to the sweet, warm air kissing her skin to the stars popping out one by one.

"Pete is the glib one in the family," Tom went on, his breath warm against her mouth. "I might not have all the right words but I'm trying to tell you I'm crazy about you. I don't want this to end when you leave tomorrow. I know we'll be on separate coasts but we'll figure something out. I can fly out to New York or fly you up to Anchorage. Maybe I can put in for a transfer to the East Coast."

Lost in the haze of growing desire, it took her a moment to register his words. When she did, fear poked at her with tiny barbs.

He was talking about the long-term here. Not a fling, not a summer romance.

What did she know about having a healthy relationship? The only example she had in her life was Sharon, with her constant string of men who changed as frequently as the daily special.

This wonderful, unbelievably sexy man was telling her he had feelings for her and all she could think was that she was bound to mess this up. She had always believed she was genetically preprogrammed to fail at love. How could she be otherwise with Sharon for a mother?

Why didn't Shelly worry about this? she wondered. Her sister was deliriously happy with her husband and child, building her dreams of forever. If Shelly believed she could make it work, why couldn't Sophie believe the same thing?

Though fear still licked at her, she pushed it away. This was her chance, her moment, and she couldn't let her mother destroy this for her, too.

She leaned across the blanket and kissed him. He groaned against her mouth and pulled her close, molding her body to him. While the waves churned against the rocks, their mouths tangled and their hands explored each other more intimately than ever before.

"I should probably mention I haven't done this very much," she said on a gasp just as his hands reached a very interesting part of her body she'd never paid much mind to before.

He stilled. "How much is not very much?"

"Um, never."

He growled a harsh oath then leaned his forehead against hers, his breath coming in ragged gasps. "You can't tell me that."

"Why not?"

"How can I take you on the beach for your first time?"

"You're a clever man. I'm sure you'll figure something out. A girl can only hope."

His laugh was rough, short. "Are you sure?"

She kissed him in answer to his question, throwing the entire force of her emotions into the embrace.

Making love with Tom on that moonlit stretch of beach had been beyond anything she could ever have imagined, sweet and tender and passionate.

Afterward, they lay in each other's arms for a long time, just listening to the ocean and the night creatures calling and peeping. She wanted to stay there forever, until she remembered she had promised Shelly she would spend at least part of her last evening with her.

Scrambling up, she hurriedly dressed.

"Can I be with you later tonight?" Tom asked. "Come to your room?"

She nodded, already anticipating a heavenly night in his arms, then she kissed him one last time and hurried for the stairs.

* * *

She had hoped to slip into her room for a quick shower before joining her sister in the nursery but the moment she walked inside the house, a door opened down the hallway and Peter stepped out.

Her sister's husband was the last person she wanted to talk to right now, with the haze of joy still surrounding her. But when he spoke to her, she knew she couldn't just ignore him.

"Sophie, I'm glad I bumped into you. I wanted to talk to you for a moment."

"I'm on my way to meet Shelly," she said warily. She wasn't sure why but something about the expression on his handsome features made her uncomfortable.

"It will only take a minute. Why don't you come into the library and sit down."

She didn't know how to politely refuse so she followed him into the richly appointed room. It was like some old-fashioned library from an English manor somewhere, with hunting prints on the walls, leather armchairs and walls and walls of books.

He gestured to one of the armchairs and without asking her preference, poured her a glass from a decanter on the desk. She took it but didn't sip, still heady from Tom's arms.

"Shelly tells me you're leaving us tomorrow."

"Yes. I have a job waiting in New York."

"What a shame. I've hardly had a chance to talk to you."

And that's just the way I like it, she thought. She had tried during this visit but couldn't bring herself to swallow her distaste for her sister's new husband.

She couldn't pinpoint exactly what it was she disliked about Peter. He seemed to adore his wife, treating Shelly like some cherished treasure.

Some probably would say he was more conventionally handsome than Tom, smooth where his older brother was rough, and she couldn't deny he could be charming in a suave, polished way.

But she still didn't like him.

"I'm sure I'll be back before you know it to visit my sister."

"You and Shelly are close, aren't you?"

"Very."

"Do you tell her everything?"

Again she felt uncomfortable at the strange expression in his eyes. "Not everything. Why do you ask?"

He shrugged and offered her a small smile over the rim of his glass. "Just wondering if you're planning on telling her about screwing my brother."

She gaped at him. "Wha—what?"

"I don't miss much. I've seen the way you and Tom look at each other. The two of you have been thick as thieves this week. Besides, I saw you go down to the beach with him and I have to tell you, I've been sitting up here the whole time you've been gone imagining what the two of you were doing down there."

Her stomach churned. In just a few words he made something that had been wonderful, magical, seem dirty and wrong. "Whatever we might have been doing is none of your business."

She stood up quickly and headed for the door but he was faster and reached it before her.

"Come on, Sophie. Don't be that way." To her horror, he reached out and traced his thumb down her jawline. "You're a beautiful woman. On the surface you look like your sister but you're different too, in some elemental, fiery way I can't quite put my finger on."

"I never asked you to put your finger—or anything else—on me."

He laughed. "You have spirit. That's one of the things I like about you."

She needed a shower desperately. A long, wickedly hot shower to wash away his touch. "I'd like to leave now. Please move."

"And I'd really like you to stay." His smile was feral. "I don't see why you can't give me some of what you're so willing to hand over to my brother."

She stared at him in shock for several seconds, trying to process how such crudeness could come out of someone who pretended to be so refined. "That's disgusting," she finally said. "You're married to my sister."

"And I love Shelly. I do. But she just had a baby and won't be cleared to have sex for weeks. That's just too long for a man like me to go without, if you know what I mean."

She was going to be sick. Nausea roiled through her, slick and greasy. "Tough. You're a big boy. You can deal with it. Buy a dirty magazine or something, but leave me alone."

"I don't think so."

Before she could react, he grabbed her arms and kissed her, his mouth hot and moist on hers. She writhed and struggled to escape but he was far stronger.

Fear flickered to life as she finally realized she might really be in danger here. Once when she was twelve or thirteen, one of Sharon's boyfriends had tried to touch her but she had been quick and wiry. She had kneed him in a particularly tender portion of his anatomy and threatened to string him up by the same body part if he ever tried to touch her again or even *thought* about trying the same thing with her sister.

That was the one time she remembered Sharon acting like a mother. Though Sophie had begged her not to, Shelly had gone straight to Sharon with the story of what the man had done. To her complete surprise, Sharon had been livid. She called the police to report the bastard and a week later they'd moved three states away.

A young, healthy man was much harder to fight off than a middle-aged, half-drunk trucker, she discovered. But Sophie had spent her childhood in rough neighborhoods where a little knowledge of street-fighting was a matter of survival.

As soon as she found an opening, she threw an elbow into his gut with enough force that his breath whooshed out of him and his hold on her loosened slightly, just enough that she was able to step away, her own breathing coming in quick gasps.

"How could you do that? You really want me to tell Shelly you attacked me when your daughter wasn't even two weeks old?"

"You won't tell her anything," he said, and she fought the urge to slap that smirk right off his face. "Because if you breathe one word of this, I'll tell her you came on to me."

"She won't believe you. Shelly knows I would never do something like that to her."

"My darling wife believes anything I tell her."

Her nausea returned. She hated the doubt curling through her. He might be right—Shelly was completely enamored of her wealthy, handsome husband. She very well might believe what he told her over what her own sister said. Sophie couldn't tell her sister any of this, she realized.

If she *did* believe her husband had attacked her sister, Shelly would be devastated. Utterly destroyed.

"Fine. We'll both forget this ever happened."

She headed for the door but again he stopped her. "I don't want to forget," he murmured. This time he backed her against the wall, his arms holding hers immobile and his body a brutally effective barrier to any of her attempts to escape.

Panic and helplessness welled up inside her as she struggled with him but his mouth and his hands seemed to be everywhere. Through the haze of pain and fear, she heard a rending, popping sound and realized he'd ripped the buttons from her shirt.

A low scream erupted from her as she fought to cover herself, to keep his hands away from her. An instant later, the door swung open and William Canfield stood in the doorway.

"What is going on in here?"

"Just having a little fun, Dad. Close the door on your way out."

"Don't listen to him," Sophie gasped on a sob, trying to hold the tattered remnants of her shirt together. "Your son tried to rape me!"

The moment the words were out, Sophie realized uttering them had been a huge mistake. Colossal. William's already stiff face turned to ice. The look he gave her was so full of venomous hatred it would have given her shivers if she hadn't already been trembling.

He took in her swollen lips and her shaking hands then looked at his son. "Peter. Leave us."

Peter opened his mouth to argue but something in his father's expression stopped him. After a pause, he walked out, closing the door to the library behind him.

As soon as he was gone, William turned to her. She almost thought she would have preferred Peter's unwanted touches to the deadly expression in William's eyes. "If I ever hear so much as a whisper of that kind of false allegation coming out of your mouth again, make no mistake, young lady. I will make you very, very sorry."

She swallowed hard at his fury. "It's not a false allegation. Your son tried to rape me. You saw me trying to fight him off!"

"I saw nothing of the sort. I saw a cheap slut trying to seduce her sister's husband."

Her insides went as cold as his eyes. "It wasn't like that. You know it wasn't."

"One brother wasn't enough for a whore like you? You had to seduce them both?"

What kind of family had Shelly married into? she wondered, teetering close to the edge of hysteria. "I didn't seduce anyone," she mumbled, wanting only to get away from him and from Peter and from Seal Point.

"I want you out of this house and I want you to stay away from my son."

"Don't worry," she snapped. "Your precious Peter is safe from me and my wanton behavior."

"The other one. Thomas. Leave him alone. I will not let the white-trash Beaumont sisters completely ruin this family. Your sister already trapped one of my sons into marriage by refusing to have an abortion after she foolishly let herself get pregnant. I'm not going to let my other son throw his entire future away on a woman like you."

This couldn't be happening. She had been so deliriously happy just a short time ago and now her world was crashing down.

"I want you out of this house now. Tonight."

She stared at him. "I promised Shelly I would be here for the baby's christening in the morning."

"Make some excuse. Tell her something came up. But I want you to leave."

Her chin went up. "And if I don't?"

"Then I'll tell Thomas and your sister both how I caught you and Peter together. I believe Shelly will forgive her husband far more readily than my son will ever forgive you."

This had to be a nightmare. People didn't act like this in real life, ordering others around, threatening them, accusing them of terrible things they knew weren't true.

She gazed at William's merciless features, knowing she had no choice but to leave. He wouldn't hesitate to lie to her sister. Her instincts told her to trust that Shelly would believe her version of the story but she knew she couldn't risk it.

Shelly was happy here, had found the very sort of home she had craved through their entire rootless life. How could she destroy that for her sister when she knew how much Shelly needed a place to nest?

Either way, if any version of this night were to reach Shelly, she would be betrayed, either by her husband or her sister. It was far better to slip away and hope the whole thing would disappear along with her.

As for Tom, she'd been foolish to let things go as far as they had, to ever believe they could share anything but momentary passion. She was Sharon's daughter, far more than Shelly had ever been, with her mother's same wanderlust and her mother's same appalling lack of self-preservation when it came to men.

Her heart shattering, she packed her things and slipped away with only brief notes to both Shelly and Tom. She hated knowing she was hurting them both but she hadn't known what else to do.

Shelly had forgiven her for leaving, as Sophie had

known she would, because she was Shelly and it wasn't in her nature to be bitter or angry. Still, the hurt had been there through the last ten years, especially when Sophie worked so hard to maintain a safe distance away from her sister and her new husband.

She had seen Shelly only a handful of times since then, the few visits she'd made here when she knew Peter was away on business and a few times Shelly had come to New York. But their relationship, already shifting and changing after Shelly's marriage, had never been the same.

As for Tom, he had tried to contact her after she returned to New York but she had avoided his calls for weeks. Finally, after weeks of evasive tactics, she had surrendered to her cowardice and had her roommate tell him she was out with her boyfriend. To her vast relief, he seemed to get the message because the calls abruptly stopped and he never tried to contact her again.

And that was that. The whole ugly story.

Sophie blinked back to the present, unsure how long she had been sitting out here in the cool night air. It had to be close to sunrise. The light had already begun to change subtly, defining the outline of the trees, the curve of the swimming pool.

She sighed, amazed that the memories of that brief time in her life nearly a decade earlier could still seem so vivid. She had never found with another man what she and Tom Canfield had shared for those few precious days.

Like it or not, he still affected her more than any man she'd ever known. She didn't want to admit it but she couldn't lie to herself, not here in the raw honesty of approaching dawn.

She had fallen in love with him ten years ago and she suddenly wasn't so certain she'd ever climbed back out.

Sophie rose on bones that seemed old and tired suddenly and slid open the door to her room again. She would need to be waking the children for school in a few hours but perhaps she could catch an hour of sleep before then.

With any luck, she wouldn't dream.

Chapter 10

Thomas was long gone in the morning by the time the children finished their breakfast and dressed for school in their smart navy uniforms and crisp white shirts.

He left her a note in his slashing, masculine handwriting reminding her he had an early morning meeting at Canfield and urging her to use Shelly's luxury SUV in the garage to take the children to school.

She had to admit, she was exceedingly grateful she wouldn't have to face him this morning. Not after their heated kiss and the even more heated dreams that had tormented her during that brief hour before her alarm bleated her awake.

She was afraid she needed a little more time and distance between them before she would be prepared for another confrontation with him.

Frustrated at her weakness where Thomas Canfield was concerned, she shoved the blasted man out of her head yet again and tried to focus on the children.

"Are you all sure you have everything you need for the day?" she asked them one last time before they all loaded into the gleaming silver vehicle. "Lunch money, homework, notes to the teacher? Anything else we've forgotten?"

"I don't think so, Aunt Sophie," Ali said. "We'd better hurry or we'll be late."

"Right. We wouldn't want that on your first day back."

As she drove through the morning traffic to the children's private school in Carmel, the twins maintained a constant dialogue about their friends and their favorite part of school and the Thanksgiving break coming in only a few weeks.

Ali spoke little except to give Sophie directions to the school. Probably nervous about returning and having to face all the inevitable questions about her parents and the violent crash that had killed them.

Poor thing. Sophie didn't know how to help her through this, what she could say to make it better. She was only grateful that at least the children didn't know about the FBI's latest suspicion that that crash might not have been accidental.

Fifteen minutes later she pulled up in front of the school, feeling very much like a soccer mom along with all the other carpool parents in their minivans and Volvos and SUVs.

"I'll be back at two-thirty to pick you up." She kissed them, wiped a smudge off Zach's nose and sent them on their way.

The twins rushed into the school building but Ali lingered by the SUV, even though a couple of girls who seemed around her age stood talking just outside the door to the school.

She waited while Ali played with the leather strap of her schoolbag, fiddled with her ponytail, bent down to tie the laces on her Docs.

Finally Sophie knew she would have to say something or she suspected they would both still be standing there by the car when the bell rang at the end of the day. "Al, are you sure you're ready to go back to school? I don't think there would be anything wrong with you taking a few more days at home if you think you need them."

"I want to see my friends. But I'm afraid everything will be different." She nibbled her lip and flashed a quick look at Sophie then looked back at the ground. "I don't want everybody to feel sorry for me. Like I'm some poor little orphan girl now."

Oh, how she wished she had a better idea what she was doing in the whole parenting department. Was it always so terribly hard? Maybe she could sign up for a class or read some books or something so she wouldn't feel so completely out of her depth.

Of course, that wouldn't help her right now, in this moment.

"You're right," she began, praying she could find the right words to help this child who had been through so much. "For a while, everything will seem different. Your friends probably aren't going to know what to say to you. I'll let you in on a little secret, Al. Even grown-ups don't always know how to talk to people after they've suffered such a terrible loss as you and the twins. They're afraid of saying the wrong thing or making you hurt worse."

Ali seemed to be listening, even though her gaze was still fixed on the ground.

"You have to be honest and up-front with your friends about what you're feeling and thinking. That's the best thing you can do. If you don't want to talk about your parents and the accident yet, if you're not quite ready, just tell them that.''

Her lip trembled. ''Sometimes I want to talk about Mom and Dad and sometimes I don't.''

''Then say that. I'm pretty sure your friends aren't going to know how to act around you for a while. You just have to show them that all you want is for them to be your friends, just like always.''

Ali was quiet for a moment, then gave her a small smile. ''Thanks, Aunt Sophie,'' she said, hitching up her bag.

Sophie kissed her for luck, then watched as Ali turned and ran to the school. She stopped and exchanged a few words with the two girls standing by the door. After a moment, one of the girls gave her a quick, awkward hug, then Ali smiled at them and the three of them hurried into the school.

Sophie stood outside the school for a few more moments, wondering if all parents felt this little clutch of apprehension sending their children into the big, bad world.

They *were* her children now. They all had a long way to go but already she could feel their hearts knitting together. She, Tom and the children were making a family, unlikely though it might be.

A family. Now there was a strange thought.

Things couldn't continue the way they had been for the past few days. She knew that, had known it even before that devastating kiss in the early morning hours. Somehow she and Tom were going to have to figure out a way to make this work. Only trouble was, she didn't have the first clue what the solution might be.

But then, maybe she ought to try to solve the problems

of the world—or at least her little corner of it—at a time when she'd had more than a few hours of restless, broken sleep.

Sophie rolled her eyes at herself and started the SUV then pulled back into traffic. She had the rest of the day to herself until the school day ended. The first order of business was shopping for some new clothes since she had only been carrying a bare-bones travel wardrobe with her when Thomas reached her in Morocco.

A big item on her long-term agenda was arranging to sublet her apartment in New York and having her belongings sent to Seal Point, but in the meantime she needed something to wear besides a few pairs of jeans and a couple of disreputable T-shirts.

Shelly had an entire vast walk-in closet full of clothes in exactly her size but the idea of wearing her dead sister's clothes, even in an emergency, was just too creepy to contemplate.

Somehow she was going to have to face the chore of packing all those things of her sister's away, but not yet. She wasn't ready, couldn't bear even thinking about it. She needed more time to grieve before dealing with Shelly's belongings.

She spent the morning in Monterey shopping for the basic necessities—underwear, socks, a few more pairs of jeans and a half-dozen sweaters and shirts. On the way back to Seal Point she drove through Monterey's historic downtown and spotted the headquarters of Canfield Investments with its gleaming windows and graceful Spanish architecture.

She was almost tempted to stop and see how things had gone for Tom on his first morning at the helm and to ask if he'd been able to learn anything about a possible motive for someone to kill Peter and Walter Marlowe.

She couldn't stop, though. That would be something a wife would do—pay a visit to her husband after a morning of shopping. It was certainly not in the job description of a former sister-in-law.

Somehow while she was wading through the minefield of their complicated relationship, she had a feeling she was going to have to keep reminding herself they were just sharing responsibility for the children, not sharing anything else.

Instead of trying to come up with flimsy excuses to see him again, she should be doing her best to figure out a way to avoid a repeat of their scorching encounter.

William and Maura were out walking, she noticed when she returned to Seal Point and pressed the remote to open the gates. She could see them just starting out along the pathway through the trees.

She smiled and waved as she drove past them toward the garage. Maura waved back but William only gazed blankly at her. What a tragic disease, she thought again. So unfair that it nibbled away at a person's mind with such relentless brutality.

In her brief experience with him, he had been a harsh, vindictive man. Cruel, even. But even though she had despised him for his behavior a decade ago, she could never wish a fate as heartbreaking as Alzheimer's on anyone, not even William Canfield.

She parked the SUV and pulled her packages from the back seat. Somehow she managed to lug them all through the house to her room in one load.

The house seemed eerily empty without Tom and the children, she thought as she nudged open her bedroom

Play the Lucky Hearts Game

and get...

2 FREE BOOKS
and a FREE MYSTERY GIFT...

YOURS to KEEP!

yes! I have scratched off the silver card. Please send me my *2 FREE BOOKS* and *FREE mystery GIFT*. I understand that I am under no obligation to purchase any books as explained on the back of this card.

Scratch Here!
then look below to see what your cards get you... 2 Free Books & a Free Mystery Gift!

345 SDL DU6U   245 SDL DU7C

FIRST NAME

LAST NAME

ADDRESS

APT.#

CITY

STATE/PROV.

ZIP/POSTAL CODE

(S-IM-08/03)

Twenty-one gets you
2 FREE BOOKS
and a **FREE MYSTERY GIFT!**

Twenty gets you
2 FREE BOOKS!

Nineteen gets you
1 FREE BOOK!

TRY AGAIN!

door. Echoing and cavernous and forlorn, somehow. She didn't like it.

She tried to shrug off her discomfort as she walked into her bedroom and set her bags on the bed but it persisted like fingernails scraping down her spine.

Her unease seemed worse in her room. Something wasn't right. She couldn't place exactly what but some instinct warned her that all was not as it should be.

Even after walking through the room, she couldn't figure out what was bothering her. Everything seemed in order, just as she had left it.

Shaking her head at her overactive imagination, Sophie went to the walk-in closet that was larger than most of the world's dwellings. An entire extended family in some third-world country could live quite comfortably in a house the size of Shelly's closet.

Peter's half of the closet held mostly crisp white shirts and suits in conservative grays and browns but her sister had always loved clothes. Her side of the closet reflected that. The colors were more muted than Sophie would have chosen but everything was tasteful and pretty.

She pushed aside some elegant cocktail dresses to clear a space for her new clothes, dreading again the thought of having to deal with the entire contents of this closet. Perhaps she could store them in one of the other bedrooms of the house, just until her psyche healed enough that she could handle poring through her sister's things.

She ought to transfer the clothes she'd brought to the closet as well, she decided. Perhaps clearing out her suitcase would be some subtle declaration to herself that she was staying, that somehow she and Thomas could make this shared custody of the children work after all.

She found her suitcase where she'd left it, on a low, upholstered bench near the door to the balcony.

The moment she opened it, her unease returned a hundredfold.

Someone had been through her things. She knew it instantly.

She had plenty of disarray in the rest of her life—she would be the first to admit that her wandering lifestyle didn't always lend itself to order—but her suitcase was one element where she insisted on strict organization. When she spent ten months out of every year traveling, well-structured packing became a necessity.

She would never have left her things jumbled like this, with shirts unfolded and her lingerie strewn across her robe and one of her favorite leather boots separated from the other.

This wasn't the way she had left it after she dressed that morning, she knew that with grim certainty. Somehow between the time she and the children had left for school and when she had returned from shopping, someone had gone through her suitcase.

She frowned, trying to make sense of it. Why would anybody want to ruffle through her things? She had little of value in here. Her camera gear was top of the line and certainly worth a tidy sum but it was packed separately in padded titanium cases. The few all-purpose clothes she traveled with should have no interest to anyone.

Who would possibly want to look through her suitcase? Beyond that, who would even have access to it? Only Mrs. Cope, the nurse and William, and what possible motive would any of them have?

William. Perhaps he had gone wandering through the house and come in here for some reason, although she couldn't imagine the competent nurse giving him that kind of latitude. If he had come in here, why would he go through her suitcase and leave the rest of the room untouched?

Or maybe not untouched.

She looked carefully around the room and began to notice things she'd missed earlier. A drawer ajar, a few things rearranged on a shelf, a landscape askew on the wall.

Maybe that's why she had been uneasy when she first came in. Though her conscious mind wasn't familiar enough with the room's contents to notice anything amiss, maybe her subconscious had been more acute.

What should she do? Should she tell someone? Tom would think her crazy if she went to him about this, especially after the night before and her mysterious phantom intruder.

She sat on the edge of the bed gnawing on her bottom lip. She had to let Tom know about this, even if he thought she was becoming paranoid. Something strange was going on at Seal Point and she owed it to her sister's memory to find out what.

How had his father and Peter survived this kind of thing day after endless day? Tom sat behind his brother's modern art sculpture of a desk, in his brother's gleaming chrome chair, and tried to to ignore the way his Hermes tie seemed to be strangling the life out of him.

Here it was barely lunchtime and he was already desperate to escape the stifling atmosphere at Canfield.

Across from him, Peter's assistant seemed to be turning the same power red as the tastefully folded handkerchief tucked into the breast pocket of his suit.

"Your brother spent months working on this deal with

Yamasaki," James Randall exclaimed. "If we back out now, we'll completely destroy a relationship he spent months cultivating."

Tom gave him a cool look, working hard to swallow his dislike for the other man. Since he had arrived at Canfield that morning, Randall had done nothing but raise objections to every decision Tom tried to make.

The man rubbed him wrong, from his artificially tight-jawed Ivy League drawl to his smooth two hundred-dollar haircut to his carefully manicured hands.

"I never said anything about backing out. I said the company should take more time to study the issues before going through with it. In light of the recent deaths of Peter and Walter Marlowe, I'm sure they'll understand that Canfield is currently in a regrouping phase."

A regrouping phase that was going to require extensive auditing to figure out what the hell Pete had been up to and why so much of the company's operating budget seemed to have vanished in the past few months.

"This is a mistake. There's no reason we can't go forward with the deal, just as Peter would have wanted."

"Margot and I agreed it would be prudent to wait until things are settled here at Canfield before going ahead with a deal that involves such a substantial amount of money."

"Margot." The sneer in Randall's voice left no doubt in Tom's mind of the other man's opinion about the acting financial officer, Margot Henley. "What does she know? She's as conservative as Walter was."

"Walter's conservative approach mirrored my father's. Together they built Canfield into the company it is today."

"And your brother's willingness to take risks nearly doubled the profit margin in just a few years."

And cost some of their investors their life savings when those risks had gone sour, Tom was learning. "I'm not my brother, Mr. Randall."

"No. You're not." The implication was obvious— Tom could never hope to fill his brother's Bruno Maglis, in Randall's mind at least.

"I'll repeat the objections I raised to the board of directors when they named you temporary CEO. Just because you have the right last name doesn't mean you should be the one running Canfield."

For once, Tom couldn't have agreed more with the man, even as he longed fiercely to be up in his Dolphin where he could toss over dead weight like Randall.

Before he decided the high-powered executive life wasn't for him, he had given in to his father's demands and obtained an MBA from Stanford, so he wasn't completely out of his league here at Canfield. He just had no desire to even step out onto the playing field.

James Randall obviously thought he should be the one sitting in this uncomfortable chair, behind this monstrosity of a desk. Was he ambitious enough to kill the man who had been in his way? Tom wondered.

"I'm sure the board of directors will take that into consideration when they meet to name a new chief executive officer in a few weeks. In the meantime, since my family still maintains seventy-five percent interest in the company, I suppose that gives me the final vote for now on things like the Yamasaki deal."

Janine, his father's secretary for years and Pete's after that, buzzed in before Randall could voice further objections. "Mr. Canfield, you have a call on line two. A Sophie Beaumont."

Sudden apprehension clutched at his stomach. Sophie never would have called him at the office unless something was wrong. "We can continue this conversation later," he told Randall.

"What am I supposed to tell Sam Yamasaki?"

"Exactly what I said earlier. Tell him to come back to us in a few weeks when things are a little more settled." At this point, with the mess Peter had left behind, that might take years rather than weeks but he wasn't about to tell Randall that.

He picked up the phone as soon as the man had left the room. "What is it? Are the children all right?"

There was a slight, startled pause on the other end of the line. "Yes. They're fine. At least I think so. I don't pick them up for another hour."

Relief rushed through him and he let out the breath he hadn't realized he'd been holding. "My father, then?"

"No. It's nothing like that. Everyone is fine. It's nothing, really. Stupid. I wasn't even going to tell you but then I thought you should know."

"What's going on?"

"Tom, I think someone's been in the house."

He sighed. "Sophie, I thought we settled this last night. Whatever you saw, it couldn't have been an intruder. I spoke with the security company this morning and the computers haven't recorded any abnormal breaches in the system."

"I'm talking about this morning. After I took the children to school I ran some errands in town and was gone for perhaps three or four hours. When I returned, I found things I believe are out of place in Peter and Shelly's room and my suitcase has obviously been searched."

He leaned back in what had to be the most uncomfortable chair in the building, all bony angles and awkward lines. It didn't surprise him at all that Pete had been willing to sacrifice comfort for fashion. "Did you ask Mrs. Cope if she cleaned there? Perhaps she was looking for laundry."

"In a closed and zippered suitcase? She's certainly efficient but I can't believe she's *that* efficient."

"But did you ask her? She's the only one besides Maura and my father with access to the house."

"No. I thought it best to talk to you first to see if you want me to contact the police."

"The police? Why would you do that? Is something missing?"

"Nothing of mine, as far as I can tell, but I don't know whether anything is missing in the house. I don't really know enough about Seal Point or its contents to know for sure. Tom, I thought perhaps this could be linked to Peter and Shelly's deaths."

Damn the FBI for raising all these fears in a woman who had always showed a reckless disregard for her own safety when it came to her photos. He still broke out in a cold sweat when he remembered the time he had taken her down Highway 1 to photograph the Point Sur lighthouse and she had decided to crouch on the lip of an eight-hundred-foot cliff in heavy winds for a better shot.

"I don't think we need to bring the police in at this point. I'm sure there's a logical explanation for it. Talk to Mrs. Cope and maybe Maura first. See what they have to say first before we do anything else."

She was silent for a moment. "Okay," she finally said. "I'll talk to them. You're probably right, I'm probably being paranoid. I'm sorry to bother you about this, especially when I know how hectic things must be there."

"Don't worry about it. It's good to talk to someone not in a business suit for a moment."

Though he had a thousand things awaiting his attention, he was loathe to hang up. It was the strangest thing. Talking with her—with Sophie, of all people—he felt centered, at peace, for the first time all day.

''The children made it to school all right?''

''Yes. Ali was nervous about how her friends would treat her but we talked it over and I think she was able to figure out how to go on.''

''I wish she didn't have to deal with all this. She's just a little girl.''

''I know. But she's strong. They're all strong, Thomas. It will take a while but they'll begin to heal.''

What would he have done if she hadn't come back? She had such wisdom and strength toward the children. He never would have expected Sophie to be such a natural at caring for them but she was warm and serene. Maternal.

He pictured her the evening before, the children in their pajamas and Sophie kneeling with them by the bed as they said quiet prayers for their parents. He never would have thought of doing such a thing but he was sure the ritual had been comforting for the children.

How could he persuade her to stay? The children needed her. She had to know that, but would it be enough?

He needed her here. He closed his eyes, remembering their erotic encounter in the darkened hallway. Her welcoming mouth and her soft skin and her eager response. He could quickly become addicted to her, just as he'd been a decade ago.

He jerked his mind from that dangerous road. If she decided to leave again, there wasn't a damn thing he could do about it.

"I'll be home late. Tell Mrs. Cope not to hold dinner for me," he said, more abruptly than he'd intended.

"Okay." She sounded startled by his harsh tone. "Sorry again that I bothered you."

She had been bothering him for a decade, he finally admitted to himself as he hung up the phone.

For ten years, Sophie Beaumont had been the one woman he could never quite forget, no matter how hard he tried.

Chapter 11

Sophie checked her watch as she headed outside into the cool November afternoon.

She had twenty minutes to talk to Maura McMurray before she had to leave for afternoon pickup at the school in Carmel. That ought to give her just enough time to determine whether William might somehow have wandered into her room and looked through her suitcase, since Mrs. Cope claimed she didn't know anything about it.

She found them digging in a flowerbed out front, a small pile of what she thought might be tulip bulbs next to them.

William had dirt ground into the knees of his khakis and what looked like a mustard stain on his golf shirt but he seemed to be enjoying himself immensely. His face glowed with color and he was smiling more broadly than she'd ever seen him do.

There was something heartwrenching, poignant, about

his transparent joy in being outside in the cool sunshine. He was like a gleeful child, just happy to be alive and outdoors.

William stopped digging long enough to lift his face to the sky and she wondered if Tom would be offended if she asked to photograph William out here where he seemed so happy.

She wasn't sure she would ever dare ask but if she did, she knew any photographs she captured would be among the most moving she had ever taken.

She walked closer and was surprised when William turned his smile at her. "Shelly. There you are. Peter was looking for you earlier."

"He…he was?" As usual, she didn't have the first idea how to handle his delusions.

"Yes. I told him you probably went shopping. I know how much you like to shop. He said he would find you later."

Before she could answer, the nurse interceded. "Look, William. We have all these tulip bulbs to plant and it's almost time to go inside. We'd better hurry."

He immediately turned back to the garden, digging quickly with the hand spade he held.

With William occupied, the nurse walked over to Sophie. "I'm sorry about that, Ms. Beaumont. I suppose I should correct him, remind him again that Peter and Shelly are gone. But he gets so agitated whenever I bring up the accident. I hate to put him through it over and over. It seems easier to let him go on believing everything is still all right."

"If it gives him some comfort to think I'm Shelly, I don't mind. And please, call me Sophie."

The nurse's plump features creased into a smile. "Sophie. And I'm Maura."

Sophie watched William place a tulip bulb in the hole he had dug with the care of a heart surgeon precisely implanting a pacemaker then he carefully tamped dirt around it. "He seems to enjoy being out here."

"We try to spend a little time every day outside. It's funny. According to his sons, Mr. Canfield was never one for gardening before the disease hit him. Never had the time, I guess. But this seems to be a kind of therapy for him now. When we don't come out because of the weather or doctor visits, he frets and stews all day about his flowers until he can come out again to make sure everything is all right."

"You're very good with him."

"It's not always easy but I enjoy it. Before this job, I worked in a nursing home wing that had a hundred patients. Now *that* was tough duty. It was so difficult to really get to know any of them with my shift constantly changing. It's truly been a unique experience to be able to devote all my time to just one patient."

The woman was dedicated and caring. How could Sophie possibly ask her if she might have let Tom's father wander around the house at will? She tried to figure out how to bring up the question but couldn't find any words that didn't sound accusatory or distrustful.

At her continued silence, the nurse gave her a concerned look. "Is something wrong?"

"I don't know. I need to ask you something. But to be honest, I'm not sure how to begin."

"Just go ahead and ask."

She took a deep breath and finally blurted out the question. "Was there any chance William might have had reason to go into Peter and Shelly's room this morning?"

Maura gasped and raised a hand to her mouth. "Oh,

no. Did he break something? I'm so sorry, Ms. Beaumont. Sophie. I'll pay for whatever he might have gotten into.''

"So he could have been in there?"

"Yes. He was watching his favorite game show in the media room. Usually he's completely engrossed in it and barely even blinks so I took a moment to talk with JoAnn in the kitchen. Mrs. Cope,'' she added at Sophie's blank look.

"I talked to her for maybe ten minutes,'' the nurse continued, ''but when I walked in to check on William he was gone. I found him in the upstairs hallway. He was very excited, going on and on about Peter again. It took me so long to calm him down that I didn't think to check the bedrooms for damage. I'm so sorry.''

"He didn't break anything.'' She rushed to allay the other woman's obvious distress. "I just found some things disturbed and was trying to figure out what might have happened. No harm done at all.''

What a relief! All this worry for nothing. She should have asked Maura first instead of rushing to Tom with her paranoid concerns that an intruder had searched her things.

Now she wished that she'd kept her mouth shut, especially after the abrupt way he had ended their phone conversation, as if he couldn't wait to be done talking to her.

"I am sorry, Sophie,'' the nurse said again. "It won't happen again, I promise. I'll watch him every moment.''

"You can't be on duty twenty-four hours a day.''

"Oh, I'm not. I'll admit, things have been a little hectic this week with the funeral and all but it's usually not so crazy. Another nurse from the agency comes once a week on my day off. Before she died, your sister helped quite a bit and even before he moved into the house, Thomas used to come several evenings a week to stay with his father.''

Still, the burden of caring for William fell on Maura's shoulders. ''You know, I have some time during the day while the children are at school,'' she said on impulse. ''I've been trying to figure out how to fill it until I decide what to do with myself. If you need an extra set of eyes on William sometime while you take a break, I would be glad to help for an hour or two.''

She was surprised how easy it was to make the offer. Why would she be so willing to help care for William, the man she had despised and feared for so long?

Maybe because this man with his hands buried in the dirt and his silver hair ruffling in the wind seemed like a completely different person from the man who had bullied her into leaving ten years ago.

Maura smiled at her. ''He would enjoy that, I think. Your sister was wonderful with him. So patient and loving. He loved to listen to her read to him. He would sit for hours and never seemed to tire of it. I swear, she went through every book in the house. Mark Twain, Shakespeare, Steinbeck. Even the children's books.''

Shelly had been such a good person. Decent and loving and kind to everyone, whether they deserved it or not. Tears burned behind her eyes. How could fate have taken someone with so much to offer the world?

''Shelly always seemed to know just what people around her needed to make them happy,'' she murmured.

That had been her sister's gift, one developed during a childhood where they had been forced to nurture each other.

''Mr. Canfield loved her like a daughter. I'm sure her loss hurts him every bit as much as losing Peter. I believe that's why he's having such a hard time accepting she's dead, why he wants so much to believe you're her whenever he sees you.''

Now that was a surprise. Sophie was sure the nurse had to be mistaken. She remembered clearly during that last terrible meeting with William how he had said Peter was throwing his life away on Shelly and accused her of trapping his son into marriage by her pregnancy with Ali. ''The white-trash Beaumont sisters,'' he'd called them.

Could he really have had such a complete turnaround in the years since?

She wanted to believe Shelly had been happy here, wanted some assurance that she had been right in the choice she'd made ten years ago to leave without destroying her sister's marriage.

If Shelly and William had been able to develop a loving relationship before he'd been struck by Alzheimer's, perhaps her sister really *had* found the home and family she had always dreamed of.

''Why don't I read to him for an hour or so tomorrow morning after I take the children to school?'' she said to Maura. ''That should give you a nice break.''

The nurse smiled. ''You're every bit as sweet as your sister was.''

Very few people in her life had ever called her sweet. She'd been the reckless twin, the troublemaker. The wild one. But she had to admit, it was nice to hear for a change, even if it wasn't true. She smiled back at Maura, grateful to have found a friend here at Seal Point, then hurried off to collect the children from school.

What a hellish day.

The house was quiet and dark when Tom returned from the office. He turned on the lights in the kitchen and found a note on the counter from Mrs. Cope, informing him she had left a plate of grilled chicken and pasta for him in the refrigerator and some Dutch apple pie on the counter.

The woman was double the worth of any of the high-priced executives at Canfield, he thought. With a mental note to give her a well-deserved raise, he dug through a drawer for a knife to cut into the crusty, delectable-looking pie when he spied a math book on the table. Ali must have been working on her homework in here.

With a sigh, he set the pie back on the counter for later. He desperately needed a hot meal and a good, hard five-mile swim to work out all the kinks in his spine and take away the tension spawned by a fourteen-hour day. But he needed to see the children first.

He checked his watch. Just after eight. He might still be in time to read them a story before bed.

On his way up the stairs, he took off his tie and hung it on the newel post, heading toward the soft murmur of voices and muted laughter. The door to the master suite was open and warm, welcoming light spilled out into the hallway.

When he peeked inside, he found Sophie sitting on the bed propped against the headboard, her legs outstretched. A twin sat on either side of her and Ali cuddled next to Zach.

She was smiling down at something Zach said and the light from the bedside lamp created a shimmering glow around her. Something funny tugged at his chest. Something rich and full and tender, and he could do nothing but stare.

He still had feelings for her. He couldn't deny them

any longer, not when they reached out like this and grabbed him by the throat.

In just a few short days he had let her sneak her way into his life, into his heart. Stupid. Utterly stupid, when she would only be leaving again, when he could do nothing to stop her, just like a decade ago. How was he supposed to stand by and watch her walk away again?

He breathed out another sigh, loud enough to catch her attention. She looked up and caught him watching her and he watched as an appealing little blush spread like spilled wine along her cheekbones.

For a few breathless seconds their gazes held. It might have been a trick of the light or wishful thinking on his part but he thought he saw something in her eyes, some answering emotion. She looked happy to see him. Almost as if she'd been waiting for him.

They stared at each other for a long moment. Everything else—the room, the children, his tight muscles and empty stomach—faded away, leaving only Sophie.

And then Zoe caught sight of him and shattered the connection by shrieking with excitement. "Uncle Tommy! You're home! You're home! Guess what? My best friend Bella broke her arm on the swings at school today and she had to go to the doctor and get a cast and everything. It's pink. She said it hurt a lot."

With effort, he slid his gaze away from Sophie and focused on his niece. "I'm sure it did."

"Yeah, and her mom said tomorrow when she comes back to school we can write our names on it and stuff."

He leaned against the door frame. "What other kind of stuff do you think you'll put on her pink cast?"

"I don't know. Maybe I'll draw a rainbow. I'm super good at making those."

Zach snorted at the idea and Tom turned to him. "How was your day, bud?"

Thin shoulders lifted inside his airplane pajamas. "Okay. We had corndogs for lunch and Tanner threw up. It was really gross."

"I bet. Al, what about you? I saw your math book down in the kitchen. Did you finish your homework?"

She shook her head. "I missed a lot of assignments. I still have a few to make up but Mr. Lindley gave me until the end of the week to turn them all in."

"I can help you if you need it. Math was one of my best subjects."

She smiled. "Thanks, Uncle Tommy."

He returned her smile, astonished at the comfort he found being here with all of them. The stress of the day already seemed to fade away, layer by layer.

How had his life managed to change so drastically? A week ago he was content with his bachelor life, living alone in his condo in Pacific Grove. He dated some and hung out with buddies from the Coast Guard and spent time helping out with his father but other than that he had had a pretty solitary existence.

That life seemed as cold and barren as the Arctic.

"How was the rest of your day?" he asked, remembering his conversation with Sophie about Ali being upset before school started.

"Good. I missed my friends a lot. It was really great to see them all again. I was afraid it would be weird but it wasn't."

Sophie gave her arm a little squeeze then turned her attention to him. "You're just in time for a story, Tom. We're reading *Green Eggs and Ham* tonight."

"Ah. One of my favorites."

"I picked it," Zoe said proudly. "It's one of my favorites, too. Do you want to hear the story with us, Uncle Tommy? You can lay here by me. I'll make room.''

Now that was a dangerous idea, sharing a bed with Sophie. On the other hand, they had three eager chaperones. How much trouble could they get into? After a moment he shrugged, slipped off his shoes and joined them all on the wide bed.

He listened to them all take turns reading, the twins halting over the words and Ali and Sophie helping them along. It didn't take long for him to close his eyes. This was nice. It was warm and comfortable and he felt more relaxed than he'd been all day....

"Tom. Thomas.''

He blinked and found Sophie leaning over him, her tousled curls brushing his face. He wanted to wrap one of those curls around his finger and tug her down to him. To roll over and cover her with his body and kiss her until he couldn't think straight...

He blinked away the thought. "Did I fall asleep?"

"I think so. Either that or you were meditating on the deeper literary nuances of *Green Eggs and Ham.*''

He sat up against the headboard. "Try it, you'll like it. I had an American Lit professor in college who believed the book was a metaphor for the whole Sixties experience.''

Her soft laughter wrapped around him like a warm breeze and another layer of his stress slid away. "The children are brushing their teeth then heading to bed.''

He shoved off the bed. "I'll tuck them in, if you don't mind, since I haven't seen them all day.''

"I don't mind.''

After prayers had been said and kisses exchanged and blankets tucked in just right, he left the twins' door ajar and returned to the hall. To his surprise, Sophie was waiting for him.

"Did you find something to eat? Mrs. Cope said she would leave a plate for you in the refrigerator. I'm sure she did. I've learned the woman doesn't say much but she backs up her words with actions. Dinner was a really delicious grilled chicken and pasta with Dutch apple pie for dessert. Zach's favorite, apparently."

It had been so long since someone had fussed over him that he didn't know quite how to respond. He had to admit, he liked it, though. "It's one of my favorites, too. I saw her note and what was left of the pie when I came home but I wanted to see the children first before they went to sleep. I guess I'll go finish it off." He shrugged. "And maybe everything else in the kitchen while I'm at it."

She laughed. "Been a long day, has it?"

"Excruciatingly."

Her laughter faded and she touched his sleeve. "I'm sorry. I know it's not easy for you, taking over at Canfield."

He was silent, warmed more than he should be by the concern in her eyes, by the frown twisting her mouth. He wanted to kiss that mouth. Wanted to taste her again, to pick up exactly where they left off the night before. Tangled mouths and straining bodies and ragged breathing. He wanted all of it.

Without thinking it through, he leaned forward slightly. She swallowed but didn't back away.

Just before his mouth descended to hers, he jerked back to his senses. He couldn't kiss her. Not when she had made it abundantly clear the night before that she wasn't any more interested in what he had to offer than she'd been a decade ago.

He checked the motion even as his body cried out in protest. "I'm going for a swim," he said abruptly.

He was starving but dinner could wait. Now he not only needed to work out the stress of the day that had somehow returned in the last few moments but the relentless desire for Sophie that burned through his insides, brighter than ever.

Chapter 12

This time when she awoke a little after midnight, Sophie only sighed with resignation.

At this rate, maybe she ought to think about trying to rustle up some kind of over-the-counter sleep aid. She hadn't had a decent night's rest since that terrible phone call from Tom in Morocco. Though she usually tried to avoid sleeping pills, sometimes they were a necessary evil when she spent her life jumping between time zones.

She certainly couldn't keep functioning on the tiny amount of sleep she was eking out each night. With another sigh, she rolled over and tried to adjust the pillow to a little more comfortable position. On this side she could see the moonlight filtering through the filmy curtains. She watched it dance across the floor, making filigree patterns on Shelly's carpet.

She supposed she should be grateful she had been able to get any sleep at all, especially since her bedtime entertainment had been anything *but* restful. For longer than she cared to admit, she had stood behind those very curtains watching out the window at Tom's powerful strokes in the swimming pool.

Was it her fault her room had such a perfect view of the pool? He hadn't helped by staying out in the water for more than an hour.

She had tried to resist as long as she could, had curled up in the comfortable armchair pretending to read a mystery she'd picked up that day on her shopping expedition.

Normally she loved the author's quirky sense of humor but she couldn't seem to focus, too busy trying to ignore the urge to sneak just a peek and unable to concentrate on anything else but the knowledge that he was out there just on the other side of the window.

Finally she had lost the battle with her own prurient curiosity. Oh, she fed herself some palatable lie about how she really ought to make sure he was all right since he'd been out for so long. Maybe he'd gotten a cramp or something. It really wasn't safe for him to be out there by himself.

Even as she'd come up with the flimsy excuse to peek, in her heart she knew she only wanted to watch him, to take this rare opportunity to catch him in an unguarded moment.

And then once she saw him out there she couldn't manage to drum up the self-control to step away from the window.

There was something captivating, seductive, about watching a well-honed athlete cut through the water with such strength and grace. He was a thing of beauty that was definitely a joy to behold.

His body had matured in the decade since her hands

had so briefly explored that firm skin. His shoulders were wider, more toned, his thighs tight with muscles.

Again she longed for her camera to catch that moment when he turned in the water and shoved off smoothly from the pool's edge to head back in the other direction.

He was beautiful. Lean and male and muscular, and her insides had been weak just watching him. That was another excuse she used to remain rooted at the window. How could she possibly move away when she was afraid her trembling knees wouldn't support her?

At last he had climbed from the pool, droplets clinging to his skin, and grabbed a towel off one of the deck chairs. He had rubbed at his face first and then dropped the towel.

For one horrible, heart-stopping moment he had looked up at her window. She had gasped and quickly stepped back from the glass, mortified that he might have seen her standing there watching him like some sex-starved voyeur.

He couldn't have seen her, she assured herself after a moment's reflection. She at least had the foresight to turn off the lights in her room and would have been concealed by the darkness and the curtain.

But still she wondered.

Though it had still been early by her usual standards when he finished his swim—not yet ten—she had decided reading would be pointless after that. How could she be expected to concentrate on words when the image of Tom soaring effortlessly through the water was etched into her mind like acid on glass?

She hadn't dared go down to the media room to watch television for fear she might run into him there. She just wasn't up to another confrontation. Not tonight.

And since she was exhausted anyway from her tumultuous night before—first that heated kiss and then the sleepless night that followed it—she decided the smartest thing would be for her to try to rest while she had the chance.

By some miracle she had drifted off quickly. But just as the night before, the few hours of rest she had managed to find had been haunted by torrid dreams of steamy kisses and sweat-soaked bodies, dredged up by a subconscious that remembered entirely too well what it was like to be in his arms.

That must have been what awakened her, this edgy need churning through her. She fought the urge to yank a pillow over her head. She barely recognized it, she was so unaccustomed to those kinds of feelings.

Sex just hadn't been an important part of her life. Besides Tom, she'd been intimate with only one man, an Italian art dealer she'd met during the year she spent in Tuscany working on a photo book.

Gianni had been charming and sweet and had adored her. She'd been in love too, whether with him or the romance of the countryside, she wasn't quite sure now, but they had spent two delightful months together, both comfortable with the knowledge that they had no future together.

That had been four years ago and she had been celibate ever since. It had never particularly bothered her before. She had just considered herself lucky that she had escaped her mother's destructive pattern of always needing a man in her life.

But this restlessness inside her was something new.

No, she realized with one of those particularly vicious self-epiphanies. It had always been there, she had just worked herself into exhaustion for years trying not to acknowledge it. She had pretended her heart was whole and intact for so long she had almost come to believe it.

No, she wasn't like her mother. Sharon always needed a man—any man—in her life.

Sophie only needed Tom.

What a mess she had created for herself. How would she ever be able to live here with him, trapped in a platonic relationship as they cared for the children? Bumping into each other in the hallway at night, sitting across from him at the breakfast table, watching him emerge from the swimming pool, wet and relaxed?

She sighed and stared up at the ceiling. She was still trying to figure it out when she heard a small, high-pitched scream.

That sounded like Zoe!

Without taking time to throw on a robe, she thrust off her covers and rushed toward the twins' room at top speed. Inside, she flipped on the light and found Zoe sitting up in her bed, her face ashen.

"What is it, honey? What's wrong? Did you have a bad dream?"

"No." Zoe sobbed. "I woked up and saw a monster. He runned out when I screamed."

Zach sat up from his own bed, rubbing at his bleary eyes. "You know there's no such thing as monsters, Zo. Mom told us."

"I saw one. He was big and mean and scary and he was standing right over there." She pointed toward the window.

"Honey, I think you were having a dream and it probably just seemed real and scary when you woke up," Sophie said gently, pulling the little girl into her arms.

"I've had that happen to me before," she went on. "One time when I was probably a few years older than you, I dreamed I had a magic cape and whenever I wrapped it around me I could fly wherever I wanted to go. Paris, New York, Rome. Anywhere I wanted. It was so real to me, I woke up with a quilt around my shoulders and your mom tugging me away from the window of our apartment.''

She had completely forgotten that little snippet of memory until just this moment, but now she could almost feel the soft cotton under her fingers and the cold rush of wind from the open window of that trashy third-floor apartment.

How significant was it that even then—when she couldn't have been older than eight or nine—she had dreamed of escape? Of flying away from Sharon and the chaos that always surrounded her.

And Shelly, as always, had tugged her back to solid ground.

''I'm sure I saw a real monster,'' Zoe insisted.

What should she do in this situation? She couldn't think of anything to make the night fears go away.

After a moment, she decided to go to the experts. Zach and Zoe knew better than anyone what made them feel better in a situation like this. ''If your mom was here, what do you think she would have done to make you feel better?''

Zoe frowned for a moment but Zach piped up immediately. ''She would probably use the bad dream spray.''

''Bad dream spray?''

''Uh-huh. It's over there on the dresser.''

Sophie rose and crossed to the dresser where he pointed. ''Where?''

''There, in the red bottle.''

The top of the dresser was cluttered with the children's treasures but she moved aside some shells and a water-smoothed piece of jade and found a fancy glass perfume bottle that looked like an antique, with an old-fashioned bulb pump spray. "What do I do with it?"

"Whenever we had bad dreams Mama would spray around the bed to keep the monsters and the scary stuff out," Zoe said. Sophie was relieved to see color return to her cheeks and her eyes begin to lose that haunted, terrified look.

"And by the windows and the door," Zach added.

"I can do that."

Though she had to admit to feeling a little foolish, she gripped the bottle and began to spray it around the bedroom. It seemed to be odorless and colorless, confirming her suspicion that it contained nothing more than water. But if it worked, she couldn't quibble. Already she could see the tension leaving Zoe.

Shelly had been such a good mother, had thrived in the role, she thought as she sprayed. How could she ever hope to measure up to her sister's example? She never would have come up with something as creative as bad dream spray.

Uncertainty and self-doubt assailed her again but she ruthlessly squelched them.

"Is that better?" she asked.

Zoe nodded. "Will you stay here until I fall asleep to make sure the monster doesn't come back?"

She sounded so forlorn that Sophie could do nothing but nod. "Of course I will, sweetheart. Do you want the light left on for a little while?"

"Yes, please."

Zoe made room for her on her narrow twin bed and Sophie leaned against the headboard and drew the little girl into her arms, tucking the quilt around her small shoulders. Zoe smelled of soap and baby shampoo and cuddly little girl. Not a bad combination at all, she thought with a contented smile.

''Will you sing me a song, Aunt Sophie? Whenever I have a bad dream, Mommy sings me the song about when the dogs bite and the bees sting until I fall asleep.''

''My Favorite Things,'' from *The Sound of Music,* Sophie realized, her heart twisting at the memory. She and Shelly used to sing that song to each other when Sharon was out late working or with her current man— or out drinking away her sorrow if she was between men.

It had been years since she'd heard it and she wasn't sure she could remember all the words but she gave it her best shot. On her second run-through, she realized Zach was already back asleep and Zoe was close. She kept singing softly and made it through one more time before she heard Zoe's breathing pattern change to a steady, even rhythm.

If only she could fall asleep as easily! Envious, she watched Zoe sleeping for a moment in the soft glow from the bedside lamp.

She looked so sweet and peaceful. How Sophie wished she could so easily vanquish all the monsters in the children's lives, with a little make-believe and a softly whispered song.

Was this how Shelly had felt watching her children? she wondered. As if she would do anything, sacrifice anything, to make their lives as smooth and trouble-free as possible?

She was trying. She would probably never be the kind of insightful, nurturing mother Shelly had been but she decided she should give herself a little more credit for effort.

She slid from the bed carefully and settled Zoe on her pillow. After a moment, she gave Zoe's forehead a soft kiss and tucked the blanket more snugly around her small shoulders, smoothing an errant curl away from her face.

A dark shadow in the doorway caught the edges of her vision as she straightened. Her mind still on Zoe's monster, she couldn't contain her instinctive gasp.

"It's me," a low voice responded. Tom, she realized. How long had he been watching her?

Nerves fluttered in her stomach but she sternly repressed them and forced herself to walk toward him. Out in the hallway, she drew the door almost closed behind her, leaving it slightly ajar in case Zoe might cry out again.

"Bad dream?" Tom asked when she joined him.

She nodded. "Zoe saw a monster."

"Poor thing. I imagine it won't be her last for a while."

"I'm sorry we woke you."

"You didn't. I was still working and heard footsteps up here. I just wanted to make sure everything was all right."

"You put in long hours, Lieutenant."

"Just for a while, I hope. The board of directors should be meeting in a few weeks to determine a permanent CEO. I've decided it's in Canfield's best interest to bring in new blood. I'll remain temporarily until the board of directors can choose a replacement for Peter."

She heard the weary resignation in his voice and knew what a tough decision that must have been for him, to seek someone outside the Canfield family to run the company for the first time in its history.

On instinct, she touched his arm in sympathy then

regretted it when she encountered heat seething from him. She quickly dropped her fingers and cleared her throat. "Will you go back to the Coast Guard?"

He shrugged. "Hard to say right now. Even if they're willing to extend my leave of absence until things are settled here and at Canfield, I'm not sure the Coast Guard would be the best place for me anymore."

"Why not?"

"I've been lucky to be stationed close to home at Monterey Bay for the past three years but I can't say how long that might last. I could be transferred out of here at any time. That's the nature of the military—you go where they send you. I'm not sure that kind of up-heaval would be the best thing for the children right now."

Tom had given this a great deal of thought in the past few days, whenever he wasn't obsessing about Sophie and her soft green eyes and her delectable mouth.

"I have to think about them first," he said. "The Coast Guard was a great career when I only had myself to think about. I loved it, I won't lie to you about that. But now Ali and the twins have to be my focus. As you pointed out the day of the funeral, who's going to care for them while I'm out playing Rescue Ranger?"

"Me! I'm going to care for them, just as I have been doing. Or is that not good enough for you? I know I'm not Mother of the Year material yet like Shelly was, but I'm learning."

"That's not what I'm saying at all. You've been great with the children. I've told you that. You've given them exactly what they need. But you have to admit that we can't keep going indefinitely the way we have been these last few days."

"Why not?"

Because I can't be in the same room without wanting you. Because I see you smile and all I can think about is tasting you.

Because you're going to leave again.

"Are you just going to forget about your photography career? Throw away everything you've worked so hard to earn?"

"No. Not completely. I don't think my choice has to be an either-or proposition, Tom. Of course I can't go back to travel photography, but that's okay with me at this stage in my life. I've been thinking about maybe teaching a class when things settle down. And even before all this happened, I had some offers to do a showing. With all the galleries in the area, I believe I should be able to find at least one somewhere that would be interested in putting my work on permanent display."

"I'm sure you could. Your photos are brilliant."

She looked so astonished by his compliment that he couldn't help laughing. "What? Don't pretend modesty with me. They *are* brilliant and you know it. You have a gift, this amazing way of finding the unique and quirky no matter what you're shooting. Yet you always treat your subjects with dignity and respect."

"That's quite an analysis, Lieutenant." In the hallway lit only by the glow of a small lamp, her green eyes were wide—startled and flattered at the same time.

For some reason he couldn't identify, he was vaguely embarrassed. He was no art critic and probably shouldn't pretend he was. "My two-cent critique, for what it's worth."

"It's worth far more than two cents. Thank you."

"You're welcome."

They stood in the quiet hallway for several moments

while the house settled around them and the children slept a thin wall away.

"I should be returning to bed," she finally said. "And you ought to be trying to get some rest as well. You have to slow down sometime, Tom, or you'll wear yourself out."

"Yeah. I probably should," he murmured, warmed by her concern. Then, unable to help himself, he reached for her.

Chapter 13

For a few seconds she stood motionless in his arms, her body as stiff and unyielding as the Big Sur cliffs. He thought for a moment she would pull away and retreat to that cool distance she maintained between them, but then slowly she softened, surrendered.

Her arms slid around him and she returned his kiss with an enthusiasm that left him breathless and aching.

He wanted her with a fierce intensity he had never experienced with any other woman. He couldn't think about anything else but sinking into her, about how he had hungered after Sophie Beaumont for a decade, how his one brief taste of her so long ago had only left him craving more.

Her mouth tangled with his, warm and soft and sweet. When he slid his tongue inside, she tightened her arms around him and tilted her head to give him easier access.

He gripped one hand around her head, tangling in the sultry honey curls, and slid his other over one hip, bunching the silky material of her nightgown in his fingers as he drew her closer.

She moaned softly in her throat, a sexy little sound that made him lose all control. Their kiss grew wild, frenzied. He needed to be closer. He was crazy with it, mindless. With their mouths and bodies still entwined, he thrust open the door behind her and backed her into her bedroom. In only a few short steps they reached the bed and he lowered her to it.

He had dreamed of her for so long. Their kiss the night before had only rekindled all those old feelings he had tried for so long to suppress. No woman had ever moved him like Sophie, had ever reached into his chest and yanked out his heart.

He reached a hand between their bodies and touched her through her nightgown. She was as perfect as he remembered, curvy in just the right places. At his touch, her gasp whispered through the room and she arched against him.

She wore some kind of loose, high-waisted nightgown that for some reason brought to mind harems and smoky incense and exotic scents like cloves and patchouli.

He really loved the things she slept in—and made a mental note to tell her so. But just now he couldn't wait for it to be gone so he could taste her, touch her.

He reached for one strap to tug it down over her shoulder. It slid easily, baring the slope of one high breast gleaming white in the moonlight. His heart pounding, he leaned down and pressed his mouth to that curve. Her hands dug into his hair and she held him close while his mouth lavished attention on her. From here he could hear her heartbeat raging in his ear, as loud and reckless as his own.

Just as he moved to draw that tight rosy bud into his mouth, she froze then gripped his arms.

"Tom. Thomas. Stop. We have to stop." She sounded breathless, as if she'd just tried to outswim a riptide.

He didn't want to stop. He wanted to bury himself inside her heated body. To forget about the heartaches of the past and find a new future together.

She wanted the same thing. He could feel her limbs quiver with need, see the dazed yearning shimmer in the green of her eyes. Even as she said the words, her hands gripped his arms tightly as if she couldn't let him go.

"Why?" His word sounded harsh, flat, and she blinked.

"Be—because." She slid away a few inches—not far, but it might as well have been as wide and unbreachable as the Grand Canyon. "You know we have to stop. We can't do this. Think of the children. If we…if we make love it will only complicate a situation that's already terribly complicated."

"This has nothing to do with the children. This is about us. About unfinished business."

"We don't have any unfinished business, Tom," she said, her voice quiet, tugging up the strap of her nightgown. She sounded resigned, almost sorrowful.

"You might not, but I sure as hell do. I'd like some answers. Like how you could melt in my arms one minute then run off without a word five minutes later."

"Please, let it go. It was ten years ago. We were both young and foolish."

He rolled to his back away from her then sat up on the edge of the bed. "We weren't so young that I didn't recognize when I was falling in love. I thought you felt the same."

She stared at him as her entire world shifted like a

house sliding down a cliff in a mudslide. Falling in love. He *couldn't* have been.

She gazed at him, the powerful, unyielding strength of him. The pearly moonlight lent a harsh cast to his face, all shadows and angles and hollows, but his image began to blur with the tears burning behind her eyes. Tears she forced back.

Why did the contrary man have to go and say something like that, destroying all her defenses in one quick swipe. He had said during that magical night on the beach that he was coming to care for her but she supposed she hadn't really believed it.

A man like Tom Canfield didn't fall in love with the white-trash daughter of a wandering cocktail waitress.

Blood rushed from her face and she was cold suddenly. She didn't really think that about herself. Did she?

Had she left so easily when William ordered her away from Seal Point because some portion of her psyche agreed with him that Tom would be better off without her, that he couldn't throw his life away on someone from her kind of background?

It was a stunning thought, one she couldn't take time to analyze just now with him watching her so intently out of those silvery-blue eyes that burned in the moonlight.

"We can't do this," she repeated, trying hard to cling to her resolve. "Circumstances are vastly different than they were ten years ago. We're different people than we were then. Older. Smarter, I hope. Besides, we have the children to think about."

"I'm thinking about them. They need a stable home."

He paused, then flipped on the lamp by the bed. In the soft glow, she saw sudden resolve on his features and for some reason butterflies began to flutter in her stomach.

"I think we should get married," he said calmly.

Now the entire state of California seemed to slide into the sea. She stared at him. "Married? Are you crazy?"

"Maybe. Probably."

"Definitely! We can't possibly get married!"

He tilted his head and studied her. "Why not? You don't already have a husband tucked away somewhere in some exotic locale you've neglected to mention, do you?"

"Of course not!"

"Then what's the problem? Think about it, Sophie. It makes sense." He leaned against the headboard, seeming to be perfectly comfortable having such an outrageous conversation. "We can't go on living in limbo like we've been doing this week."

"Why not? Except for a few little glitches, it's working so far. Not great, maybe, but okay."

He made a strangled sound that could have been a laugh or a groan. "Only because I'm living on cold showers and fifty laps in the pool. Tonight only demonstrated once again that sooner or later we're going to give in to this heat between us."

"Not necessarily," she muttered.

"You keep kidding yourself, Sophie, if it helps you sleep at night. But if you're honest you'll admit that as long as we live under the same roof, it's going to happen between us. We're going to make love."

"Then I'll move out."

"And go where?"

She raised her palms in the air. "Somewhere nearby, maybe. Pacific Grove or Carmel. I don't know."

"And have what kind of relationship with the children?"

She didn't know how to answer, how to work their way out of this tangled situation.

"We both want to be involved in raising the children," he went on, "but the logistics of that are staggering if we live separately."

"Divorced people do it all the time. We could work out some custody arrangement."

"Do you honestly think having the kids spend a week with me and a week with you would be in their best interest especially now when their life has just fallen apart?"

She gazed at him helplessly. "But marriage. That's a fairly drastic step, don't you think? We can't base a successful marriage on physical attraction alone."

"Yeah, but you have to admit, it's one hell of a physical attraction. And we have the children in common. That's more than most people who get married."

She drew in a shuddering breath. Her insides were hollow, shaky, and she couldn't seem to get enough air. "You're crazy," she said again.

"What other options do we have? You've been good for the children. They need you in their lives."

Resolute determination gleamed in his eyes and his features hardened. "But they need me, too. I'm not about to let you take them and walk away from here the next time you get itchy feet. I'll fight you with everything I have before I let you do that. We're stuck, Sophie. We can't just go our separate ways and we certainly can't continue as we have been, circling around each other, trying to ignore the heat between us."

"And you think marriage is the answer?"

"I think we could make it work. What other option

do we have? Somehow we have to find a way to cobble together what's left of this family, for the sake of three children who have lost everything.''

She blew out a breath, at a complete loss for words. This was all too huge, too overwhelming. Marriage to Tom. Trying to build a life together, for the sake of the children.

It sounded like Heaven and hell, all wrapped into one staggering package.

''Just think about it, Sophie.'' He rose from the bed and crossed to the door. ''That's all. Think about it.''

Her emotions battered, numb, she watched him walk out of the room, closing the door quietly behind him.

Think about it, he said.

As if she would be able to do anything else!

They tiptoed around each other—and his impromptu proposal—for the rest of the week.

Neither of them referred to it again whenever they saw each other—which wasn't that often, between his hectic schedule at Canfield and trying to meet the needs of the children. But it was always there, simmering between them like a kettle full of something they were both afraid would explode in their faces at any moment.

The words had come tumbling out of the blue, he acknowledged in his office Friday afternoon, but the more thought he gave the idea, the more it made sense.

He couldn't let her walk away again. The children needed her too much, were blooming under her care. Grief still cut through the house like a thick, murky stream, but under Sophie's watch, Alison and the twins were learning how to navigate it, to flow with the current of their emotions instead of fighting them at every turn.

On his own, he feared they all would have floundered.

He wasn't good with emotions, probably because he'd grown up in a household where excess sentiments of any kind simply weren't permitted.

He wouldn't have known how to comfort Zoe after a bad dream or talk to Ali about how much she missed her mother or share knock-knock jokes with Zack until he stopped brooding. Sophie did all that and more.

He probably could have figured out a way to muddle through without her but he didn't want to. The children needed her laughter and her softness. She was the heart and soul of their makeshift little family.

He only hoped she was giving his proposal serious thought because he couldn't seem to focus on much of anything else, despite the tangled mess of Peter's affairs he didn't seem any closer to unraveling.

She had to say yes soon because he needed all his powers of concentration to figure out what the hell kind of mess his brother had dug for himself.

Something was rotten at Canfield. He could smell it, a lingering decay in the air that permeated everything. So far he hadn't been successful at figuring out what was wrong. According to the books, the company was exceeding income projections for the year.

But if that was the case, why had so many of their investors lost so much in the past twelve months? Where was the money coming from?

His father and grandfather had built Canfield slowly, steadily, by making conservative investments in start-up companies they believed in, with people they trusted.

Poring over the records showed him that in the three years since he'd taken over, Peter had used a very different approach. He'd taken some wild leaps, backed some risky ventures. Some investors had lost a great deal of money, something not so unusual given the uncertain economy. But while investors seemed to be suffering an endless series of setbacks, Canfield's financial picture continued rosy.

At least until the last six weeks or so, when several funds had been mysteriously depleted.

He had hired one of the best teams of accountants he could find to help sort out what Pete had been up to but so far they were stymied.

"Excuse me, sir." Janine White, Peter's efficient secretary, buzzed in suddenly. Her voice sounded tight, a few octaves higher than normal. "There are some FBI agents here to see you."

Herrera and Washburn, he was willing to bet. Good. Maybe he might finally get some answers, at least regarding Peter and Shelly's deaths. "Show them in, Janine."

The two agents who had come to Seal Point entered immediately, Herrera in the lead. He rose to greet them, his hand outstretched. "Agent Herrera, Agent Washburn. I'm glad you're here. I had planned to call you in the next day or so if I didn't hear from you about the status of the investigation. Please, have a seat."

They complied. "Thank you for seeing us so promptly, Mr. Canfield." Again, Agent Herrerra took the lead in her cool, competent manner. "We wanted to let you know that we believe we have a lead in the Marlowe hit-and-run."

"Oh?"

"The Monterey police have a suspect in custody on unrelated charges who we believe might be connected to the case. A neighbor of Mr. Marlowe's who has been away since the night of the hit-and-run finally returned to the area and learned what happened. He came forward with a partial license plate of a suspicious vehicle he had noticed in the area the night of the accident. We were able to trace it to a man named Leo Harris, who was wanted on an outstanding warrant.''

Some tiny flicker of memory sparked at the name but he couldn't place why it seemed familiar. Not surprising, he supposed. He'd been through hundreds of files in the past few weeks, so many that all the names had begun to blur together in his mind. The man's name could have been on any one of them. Or none at all.

''What do you know about him?''

''Harris has a fairly lengthy rap sheet—assault, robbery, weapons violations. Mostly penny-ante stuff, but he's been in and out of the system most of his life.''

''A partial license plate doesn't sound like much evidence to pin a hit-and-run death on.''

''We have other evidence we're not prepared to make public at this time.''

''But you think he's the man who killed Walter?''

''We're still investigating,'' Washburn hedged. ''At this point, we can only say we believe he's a definite suspect. We haven't been able to shake his alibi witnesses yet but we're working on that.''

Herrerra spoke up. ''We *can* tell you we found some blood evidence on the fender of Harris's vehicle that tentatively matches Marlow's type. We've sent it away for DNA testing but that will take a few weeks.''

''What about Peter and Shelly's crash? Any link between this Harris and their deaths?''

''We're working on it,'' she said. ''In fact, that's why we're here. We're looking for a motive. We'd like to check company records. These are tough financial times and a lot of people have seen their investments hit the toilet over the last few years. We'd like to know if Harris might be one of them or if he might have ties to any unhappy customers.''

Tom thought of all the Canfield investors who had lost money since Pete took over the company. The list of suspects would be staggering. ''Murdering three people over an investment that goes sour seems a fairly extreme reaction to a market downturn.''

Candace Herrera's smile was hard. ''When millions of dollars are involved, Mr. Canfield, no reaction is too extreme.''

He couldn't dispute that. ''Walter's replacement might be the best place to start. Margot Henley has been here for years. She knows a great deal about the inner workings of the company and she also knows her way around the computer system.''

He didn't add she was one of the few people left at Canfield he trusted implicitly.

He rose and led them down the hall to Margot's office. After he explained what the agents were looking for, she was eager to help.

''Walter was my friend. My mentor,'' she said simply. ''If someone killed him, I'll do everything I can to help you find out who.''

Tom hovered for a while but quickly realized his presence was superfluous so he decided to return to his own office. On his way, he passed Janine's desk.

''What was that all about?'' she asked.

He stopped at her desk, struck with the realization that he should have asked her to help with the research before sending the FBI agents to Margot. Janine had been with Canfield as long as he could remember, first as secretary to his father then to Peter.

A plump, proficient woman with graying hair and pictures of her grandchildren on her desk, she had doted on him and Peter when they were boys. She always used to keep Hershey's Kisses in her desk just for them on the rare ocassions they visited their father at work.

It probably wasn't a very kind thought to have about his brother but he had always been a little surprised that Pete hadn't let Janine go and hired someone polished and elegant to be his secretary.

Maybe his brother still had a soft spot for Hershey's Kisses. Or maybe Pete had just been smart enough to realize Janine was the real driving force behind Canfield.

She had been the first to point out to the family that William's behavior was becoming more and more erratic. If not for Janine's concern, they might not have noticed anything unusual for months or even years. They wouldn't have been able to get help for William so early, medication that had helped delay the progression of the disease to some extent.

He sat on the edge of her desk and decided to do a little sleuthing. He didn't want to alarm her unnecessarily so he opted not to tell her the FBI's suspicions about a possible link between Walter Marlowe's death and Peter and Shelly's crash into the Pacific.

"They're trying to find information about a man who might have been a Canfield client. Does the name Leo Harris ring any bells?"

She frowned. "Leo Harris. Actually, yes. I believe he called for Peter several times in the week before the crash. He seemed very determined to talk to him but your brother made excuses every time he called."

Tom stared at her, stunned, and realized he hadn't really expected her to know anything. Harris had called Peter? What business would a criminal like Harris have had with his brother? *Had* he been an unhappy investor? One angry enough to kill over his losses?

"Are you sure about this, Janine?"

"It's my job to remember names, Thomas," she said primly. "But I can certainly double-check for you. I log every call on the computer, with the date, time and the name of the caller. It should be on the log."

He wanted to kiss her for her somewhat frightening efficiency as he watched her call up a window on her computer then scroll back through the dates.

"It would have been around the twenty-fifth of October that he started calling," she said. After a moment of perusing the file, she frowned. "Now that's certainly odd."

"What's wrong?"

"I don't forget names. I just don't, especially when a caller is as irate as Mr. Harris was. I know I'm right about the date he started calling—it was my granddaughter's birthday and I wasn't in the mood to take any guff—but his name isn't here."

She scrolled down. "Or the next day. Or the next. How can that be? I know I'm not going crazy. It's almost like someone deleted any record that he called."

He shifted on the desk, uneasy all over again. "Who would have access to your computer?"

"I don't know. My files are password-protected but I suppose anyone with a little knowledge could have hacked in." She lifted her concerned gaze to his. "Peter knew my password, of course, in case he needed to find something on my computer when I wasn't here. But what possible reason would he have to alter the call log?"

Now there was a damn good question.

Pete, what the hell were you up to?

Why would Leo Harris have tried so frequently to reach his brother? And why would Peter want to hide that? What business might they have had together that could have been worth killing over?

He had a strong suspicion that if he or his team of auditors was able to get to the bottom of all this, he wasn't going to like what they found.

Chapter 14

"Aunt Sophie, Aunt Sophie. Look!" Zach exclaimed. "Grandfather found an invisible fish. Come see!"

Zach and William crouched near a tide pool, their heads bent together as they studied the inhabitants. Sophie snapped off a half-dozen frames of their matching gleeful face in the dusky slanted light of early evening with the stunning azure sea as a backdrop then forced herself to step away from the camera and tripod.

She wanted to stay there and take more pictures of them before the light faded. But she was trying to force herself to walk away from her camera a little more, to experience life instead of only watching it and recording it. It was tough to break habits she had worked to develop over a lifetime but she was trying.

As she moved to join William and Zach, her tennis shoes skidded over the wet, slippery rocks that rimmed the south edge of the small Seal Point beach. She teetered a little but caught her balance and hopped to the rocks where they stood looking into a small pool left by the receding tide.

She craned her neck but couldn't see anything. "Where?"

William pointed into the water. After several more moments of searching, her eyes finally picked out a small creature about five inches long nestled against a jagged rock.

"Wow! You're right, Zach. It is almost invisible. I can hardly see it, it's camouflaged so well. William, however did you find it?"

Tom's father looked pleased. He beamed at her with the same enthusiasm stamped on his grandson's face. "I don't know. I just looked and saw it hiding there. It's a cling-fish."

What kind of cruel disease left him with that tiny, seemingly insignificant snippet of knowledge while he frequently couldn't remember his own son's name? She ached again for Tom's loss. First his mother, then his brother, then this endless, painful parting with his father.

"A cling-fish, huh?" Zach said. "That's a good name. I guess that's why he's holding on to that rock so tightly."

William nodded. "A cling-fish can be stuck so tight to a rock that the current can pull the rock away with the cling-fish still holding on. Oh, and look." He pointed to a tiny pink cluster. "That's called a Hopkin's rose."

"What a pretty plant," Sophie said.

"It might look like a flower but it's not. It's really a nudibranch—a sea snail without a shell."

"How do you know all this?" she asked, baffled at the strange workings of his mind but pleased by the admiration in Zach's eyes as he looked at his grandfather.

"I just do. I've read a lot."

"It's wonderful knowledge." She peered into the water and saw other creatures she had missed earlier. "You know, I would love to come down here and photograph the tide pools again if you were willing to help me identify what's inside. Would you like to do that?"

William's shoulders, usually stooped and bent, straightened slightly. He smiled at her with a pride and dignity she hadn't seen on his features since she arrived back at Seal Point. "I would be honored to help you, Sophie," he said formally. "Anytime. Just ask."

She returned his smile, aware this was the first time since her return to Monterey that William had managed to call her by her own name instead of her sister's. Maybe all the time she had spent reading to him during the past week was paying off and he was beginning to realize his daughter-in-law was gone.

"Girls, come see all the cool things your grandfather found," she called to Ali and Zoe, busy building a castle from damp sand and ice-cream buckets up the beach a few dozen yards.

The girls abandoned their construction efforts and joined them, climbing over the slippery rocks with such alacrity that Sophie was once more glad she had trusted her instincts to take advantage of the low tide and mild weather to bring them all down to the beach.

They needed this, all of them. The twins were always happy to be outside and Ali had been upset after school. Though she hadn't wanted to talk about it, Sophie gathered one of the other girls had said something thoughtless about her parents.

Whatever the reason, no trace of her tears remained now as they all enjoyed the sunshine and moist sea air.

She couldn't help thinking it was good for the children to spend time with their grandfather, to see a side of him that wasn't confused and delusional. Sophie watched as William continued to point out the inhabitants of the tide pools, some so tiny they could hardly be seen. The children soaked up the knowledge.

"That's so cool, Grandfather," Ali exclaimed with a grin when William pointed out a miniscule hermit crab scuttling across the sandy bottom of a pool.

They were so engrossed in what he was showing them that no one noticed when Sophie stepped away and returned to her camera. How could she ignore the chance to capture such a touching scene? A grandfather passing on his dwindling knowledge to another generation before it all completely slipped away?

If nothing else, she wanted the pictures for herself so she could remember this evening.

For the next half hour she photographed William and the children while the sun continued its long, slow slide below the water. As she clicked frame after frame of the four of them, she was aware of a curious contentment stealing over her, an easy peace in her soul that had been missing for longer than she could remember.

No, not missing. She'd never had it before.

It felt right being here with them all. They belonged together, even William.

How strange was that, that she could even consider him part of her little family after their shared history? All her resentment toward him had disappeared long ago, she realized. He was part of their little makeshift family, too.

The only one missing tonight was Tom.

The thought of him sent nerves scrambling through her and she paused in the middle of changing film. She closed her eyes. Tom. What was she going to do about Tom?

All week long—as she'd gone about the business of taking the children to school and reading to William and letting her contacts in New York know her new address—she had been unable to think about anything but his crazy proposal.

Marriage. How could she marry him? She wanted the man she married to love her and trust her completely. Tom had told her he had feelings for her a decade ago but what about his feelings now? She knew he desired her but she'd seen enough of Sharon's relationships based on little more than sex to know they wouldn't last long.

Could Tom ever forgive her for leaving, enough that he would let himself love her?

He didn't trust her. She knew it—and how could she blame him for that? She had hurt him by leaving and he was not the sort of man to let someone have the chance to kick him twice. She was sure he would be doubly careful to protect his feelings around her, given their past.

Again, she couldn't really blame him but she also didn't know how they could possibly build a marriage under those circumstances. Not when she accepted that she already loved him and would be destined for heartache, spending the rest of her life pining for the love of a man who couldn't return her feelings.

But he was right; they couldn't continue with this awkward arrangement. They would have to figure out something soon but she was afraid she was no closer to knowing what that might be than she had been days ago.

She finished loading the camera and snapped the film cover back into place. Just as she leaned down to change lenses so she could frame a close-up of Zach and Zoe together, she heard footsteps clattering down the wooden stairs leading from the house.

Her heart stuttered and she turned her head, already knowing whom she would find there. She wasn't at all surprised to see Tom hurrying down the stairs toward them, looking confident and athletic and gorgeous in the waning light.

He must have changed after returning from Canfield— instead of the elegant charcoal business suit and burgundy tie he had been wearing when he left the house early that morning, he wore faded jeans and a soft cream fisherman's sweater.

She had to admit she found the contrast between the light sweater and his dark hair and the five-o'-clock whisker growth shadowing his features as sexy as the business suit had been.

He carried a basket, she noticed, and a blanket over one arm, just as he had the night they had come down here together a decade ago. Her stomach began a long, slow roll at the memory and she could focus on nothing but him and his outrageous proposal.

She straightened from her camera as he reached the bottom of the steps and fought the urge to press a hand to that stomach as he walked across the sand toward her.

"Mrs. Cope thought the troops might be starting to suffer hunger pangs. She sent me down with dinner," he said.

"The tide is starting to come in again. I think the fun down here is just about over."

"I guess I missed it all."

"If you hurry, you might still have time to explore a tidepool or two." She smiled. "I'm fairly certain the children will be willing to share their expert guide with you."

He paused from setting the blanket and basket on a fallen log behind her to glance at the figures huddled over some rocks several dozen yards away. Surprise flickered in his silvery eyes when he realized what she meant. "Dad's the expert guide?"

"He's been amazing! You should see him, Tom. He seems to know every kind of marine life down here."

The quick surprise on those masculine features settled into pensive lines. "I guess I shouldn't find that so astonishing. Dad loved the ocean. Studying it was one of the few hobbies I remember him having besides golfing at Pebble Beach and Spyglass. I suppose some of that knowledge has managed to stay with him, despite his disease."

"I think it's wonderful. The children are fascinated by this side of their grandfather."

He settled on the log next to the blanket, stretching out his long legs. "I should have thought to bring them all down to the beach together before now."

He was quiet for a moment, then he laughed a little. "I'd forgotten this but he used to bring Peter and me down on the weekends to see how many kinds of sea creatures we could each document in an hour. It was always a pretty intense competition."

"You didn't like to lose?"

He shrugged. "I didn't really care. To me, the reward was just being outside, spending time with Dad. He was a busy man when we were growing up and we didn't see much of him, so those Sunday mornings together meant a lot."

The laughter in his eyes faded. "Pete took it all fairly seriously, though. He played to win, whatever he did. If he wanted something, he wouldn't let too many things stand in his way."

She certainly knew that all too well. She shivered, remembering groping hands and scotch-scented breath against her ear.

Thomas noted her shiver but couldn't know the reason for it, of course. "It's getting chilly. Here, take this."

With a concern that nearly made her cry, he wrapped the blanket he'd brought from the house over her shoulders. She let him, aware she couldn't tell him she wasn't really cold, just walking a particularly grim route down memory lane.

"Thank you," she murmured.

He made room for her on the log and they sat in a companionable silence for a while, listening to the waves slap against the rocks and the children's low voices.

She decided not to disturb the peace of the moment by words, not when she could almost see the tension seep from his shoulders as the sun finally disappeared below the horizon.

"I needed this," he murmured. "Just to sit for a while beneath the sky."

"Rough day?"

He opened one eye. "Yeah. Yeah, it was." He paused and she was sorry she had asked when some of the tension returned. "Agents Herrera and Washburn came to visit me again today. They might have a suspect in Walter Marlowe's death."

"That's good news, isn't it?"

"Maybe. Maybe not. The man in custody might have had some business dealings with Peter."

"What kind of business?"

"There's the rub. We can't find any sign of the man in any of the files. So whatever connection he had with Peter, it either wasn't related to Canfield or wasn't anything official."

"Are you worried Peter was in some kind of trouble?"

"To be honest with you, I don't know what to think. Things are a mess at Canfield. Shoddy bookkeeping, inaccurate records. Missing escrow funds. Things were a hell of a lot easier in my life when all I had to worry about was my next mission."

"I'm sorry."

He gave her a rueful smile. "Yeah, me too." He gestured toward her camera and tripod. "How about you? I see you lugged your equipment down that long flight of stairs."

"I'm just trying to stay in practice. I haven't touched a camera in a week and my fingers were starting to itch. Your father and the children make good subjects."

"I'm sure they'll be happy to be your subjects anytime you need to burn a few rolls of film."

"Actually, that's something I wanted to discuss with you. I need to return to New York."

She was surprised to see what looked like resignation in his eyes, but maybe that was only a trick of the fading light.

"When?" he asked, his voice flat.

"I don't know. We can talk about it."

He gazed out at a small group of sea otters nearly hidden in strands of kelp a hundred yards from shore. "The board is meeting next week to pick Pete's replacement, which should take a lot of the pressure off me. After that, I should have far more time to spend with the children. Do you think you can wait a while before leaving?"

"Of course. Or I have a better idea. New York is magical during the holidays. If you think you could get away, I can put my trip off another week or so and all of us could go in early December for a long weekend. I think the diversion would be good for everyone. You could take them Christmas shopping and sightseeing while I clear out my apartment and take care of some business with a few of my editors. I only need a few days, just long enough to arrange for my things to be shipped here and to get out of my apartment lease. I've got friends who would do it for me but I'm not sure I'd trust years' worth of slides to someone else.''

He tilted his head and narrowed his gaze at her, clearly surprised at the idea. It took her a few beats to realize why—he must have thought she planned to leave for good.

Hurt washed over her like the sea cresting the rocks. If she needed any evidence that he still didn't trust her, he had just handed her plenty. Would he ever trust her? she wondered. Or would he always be waiting for her to leave?

''You thought I planned to head off to New York and not come back, didn't you?'' she asked quietly.

''I'll admit, the thought crossed my mind,'' he finally admitted.

''I'm not going anywhere, Tom. I don't know what I can do to convince you of that.''

''Marry me.''

She drew in a shaky breath, not at all sure she wanted to get into this again with him.

''I haven't pushed you.'' As he spoke, he focused on the water and the distant otters again. ''I promised myself I would give you all the time you need to consider it. But I wanted you to know I haven't changed my mind, even though we haven't talked about it again. I still think it would be the best thing for everyone.''

She thought of all the reasons why they shouldn't

marry, why she would only be setting herself up for heartbreak like the hundreds of times she had seen her mother go after the wrong man.

But Tom wasn't the wrong man for her. He was exactly right, if only they could move beyond the past and be willing to work together to build a future for the children.

She shifted her gaze to Ali and the twins, then to William. They were her family now. All of them. She couldn't imagine being happy somewhere else, without them in her life.

And especially without Tom. The thought left her chilled, despite the blanket wrapped around her shoulders.

She drew a deep breath, her stomach hollow, trembling, feeling as if she was poised on the edge of one of those jagged rocks, ready to dive into the surf. "I...okay."

He jerked his gaze to her in the fading light, his jaw sagging. "Okay? Okay what?"

She couldn't believe she had actually agreed, that the word had actually spilled out, but she knew she couldn't yank it back now.

"Okay, I'll marry you." She said the words quickly, afraid if she didn't, she would change her mind, would surrender to all her instincts that shouted at her to grab her camera gear and escape from those silvery eyes and those broad shoulders and the devastating pain she feared waited for her if they went through with this.

"You're right," she went on, staunchly ignoring those instincts. "The children need stability. Zoe's still having nightmares nearly every night and Ali cried for twenty minutes when she came home from school today and wouldn't tell me why. They try to hide it but they're frightened about the future. We need to do everything we can to give them a safe, solid home, even if it requires sacrifices from both of us.''

He gave a harsh-sounding laugh. ''Not a very flattering assessment of how you view marriage to me.''

She turned toward the children and William so Tom wouldn't be able to see the yearning in her eyes, all the emotion she would have to be so careful to conceal from him.

''This isn't a love match. We both know that. It's a pragmatic solution to a sticky custody dilemma, that's all. That said, I think it's the most sensible thing we can do.''

Tom fought the urge to shake her until she stopped talking about sensibility, pragmatism. He didn't want to hear that from her. He wanted her to be thrilled at the idea of marrying him—to fling herself into his arms and give him the answer to his proposal with passionate kisses and words of undying love.

He was so pathetic.

Head over heels in love with a woman who viewed marriage to him as nothing more than a down-to-earth answer to a difficult situation.

''When?'' he asked.

Her shrug lifted the blanket he had tucked around her shoulders. ''I don't know. I hadn't thought that far ahead. As soon as we can arrange it, I suppose.''

''How about next Friday? A week from today? That should give us time to work out all the details.''

He thought he saw panic flicker in her green eyes briefly but it disappeared so quickly he couldn't be sure. ''Next week would be fine,'' she said after a moment. ''And perhaps we can go to New York the following weekend to tie up all my loose ends.''

He agreed and they spent a few more moments discussing details that needed to be decided. The entire time they talked, he was aware of a curious sense of detachment, disillusionment.

He should be thrilled she'd agreed. It would solve many of their problems, make life much easier all the way around. The whole thing had been his idea, after all, and he had spent a week convincing himself it would work out.

So why did it leave him feeling so cold?

Chapter 15

Her wedding day dawned stormy and cheerless.

Half-dressed, her stomach a bundle of knots, Sophie stood at the window of her room gazing down at the churning gray sea far below. The weather matched her mood, she had to admit.

She felt as restless and wild as that white-capped ocean, as dark and grim as the sky full of clouds.

She couldn't stop thinking she was about to make a grave mistake, the biggest of her life. What was she doing, binding herself to man who didn't love her and couldn't trust her?

How much more joyful this day would be under different circumstances, if Tom wanted to marry her out of love, because he couldn't live without her, instead of because of their shared obligation to the three children they both loved.

She pressed a hand to her stomach. No use dreaming of the impossible. She had made her choice and now she must live with it, no matter what sort of heartache awaited her.

Still, she couldn't seem to force her muscles to move from the window and the tumultuous view below. She had never been paralyzed by nerves before—not even the time she'd been cornered by an old, wounded lion in the Serengetti—but she was still standing there with her fingers pressed against the cold glass of the window twenty minutes later when Alison and Zoe burst into the room.

"You're not ready, Aunt Sophie," Ali exclaimed. "Mrs. Cope sent us to tell you the limousines are here to take us to the courthouse. Zach and Uncle Tommy are leaving now. You have to hurry!"

She gazed at the girls in their matching lavender tulle dresses, their hair elaborately piled high on their heads and their sweet faces glowing with excitement.

Sophie had wanted a small, quiet ceremony, just her and Tom with none of the typical wedding accouterments. But after they told the children about the wedding, Ali and Zoe immediately threw themselves into making plans—helped along in large part by two devious helpers, Maura and Mrs. Cope.

Unable to figure out a way to break free without hurting everyone, she had been carried along on the tide of their excitement. So now she had two beautiful bridesmaids, a bouquet and a far more traditional wedding than she'd ever expected.

"You have to huwwy, Aunt Sophie," Zoe repeated her sister's exclamation.

This was for them, she reminded herself. Her nerves didn't matter, not if this marriage would help the children ease into a new life without their parents.

"You're right." She reached for the dress the girls

helped her settle on after three days of shopping, a creamy, softly romantic creation with seed pearl buttons and an empire waist they had found in a boutique in Capitola. She pulled it over her head and the material fell in soft folds to midcalf.

"Here. Help me with the zipper, will you?"

Her little bridesmaids were quick to step forward. With solemn expressions that made her smile despite her nerves, Ali worked the zipper while Zoe went to work straightening the lines of the dress.

When they were finished, Sophie gazed at herself in the full-length antique mirror near the fireplace. She didn't recognize the pale stranger staring back at her with the elegantly coifed hair and the fine-boned features and the eyes that looked far too big for her face.

"You look beautiful, Aunt Sophie," Ali declared.

"As pretty as Mommy," Zoe added.

Ah, Shelly. A deep sense of loss settled in her chest. If she had ever bothered to dream about her wedding day, she would have pictured Shelly right there, fussing over her. Fixing her hair, whispering advice, crying over every little thing, as Shelly often did.

She never would have dreamed she would be getting married without her sister there to help her through it or that Shelly's death would be the impetus behind the whole thing.

Her sister's children needed a stable home, a family, and she would do her best to give them that. No matter the cost.

With another deep breath, she pasted on a smile for the girls and reached for their hands.

"Let's go have a wedding," she murmured.

Despite her resolve, the trip to the courthouse had a hazy, unrealistic feel to it, as if she watched everything around her through a Vaseline-blurred star filter.

The girls chattered animatedly through the entire drive. She tried to focus on them but couldn't seem to concentrate on much of anything but the nerves in her stomach. Before she knew it, the limo pulled up in front of the historic Monterey courthouse, where they were greeted by an eager law clerk the moment the driver opened the door.

"This way. They're waiting for you." The fresh-faced young woman seemed to be bubbling with as much excitement as the girls. "We're all so thrilled about this. Judge Philips doesn't have the chance to perform many weddings."

The judge was a friend of William's. Since neither she nor Thomas felt right about a church wedding under the circumstances, they had agreed a courthouse ceremony would be best, despite the nudging of Maura and Mrs. Cope.

By the time the clerk led them through an echoing marble hallway to a door identified as Judge Coleman Philips's chambers, her nerves were stretched to the breaking point and she was horribly aware her hands were perspiring as she clutched the little bouquet she and the girls had picked that morning from the Seal Point gardens.

The clerk pushed open the door and the dozen or so people in the room fell silent. She saw Maura and Mrs. Cope before her gaze landed on Thomas, standing with Zach near a dignified balding older man she assumed was the judge.

Her groom wore his Coast Guard dress uniform and the honors and insignias pinned to his chest gleamed under the fluorescent lights. He looked handsome and strong and solid, the most solid thing in her universe suddenly, and she wanted to cling to him until the room stopped spinning.

He smiled at her, his eyes warm. Somehow just that brief connection helped her find her center. She smiled back and relaxed her fingers on the bouquet.

"This must be your lovely bride," the judge said. "Shall we get started, then."

"By all means," Tom said and held out his hand to her.

It was done. They were married—Sophie was his wife.

His stomach clenched at the word. How far had he come, from a Coast Guard chopper pilot content with his bachelor life to a man with a wife and a ready-made family?

How could his world change so completely in only a handful of weeks?

And Sophie. How did she feel about all of this? He couldn't read her at all. She veiled all her emotions behind a bright smile.

She looked radiant just now across the room as she bent down to say something to the children. She clutched the small spray of flowers he knew came from the Seal Point gardens and they were a vivid splash of color against her pale dress.

She looked lovely. Demure, in an un-Sophie-like way, but lovely, with all that sensuous hair piled onto her head. She was luminous, vibrant, like a spear of sunlight cutting through the water on a gray day.

For one crazy second, he wished this was a regular wedding, that they were two people in love preparing to begin their lives' journey together. The fierceness of his desire startled him.

"She's a beautiful bride," Coleman Philips murmured, following his gaze. "You're a lucky man, Thomas."

Lucky? He thought about the word. Given their circumstances it shouldn't have fit, but somehow it did.

He *was* lucky.

Sophie was willing to sacrifice everything—a successful career, her home, her wandering lifestyle—to help him care for the three children they both loved.

"I only wish your father could be here to see his oldest son wed," the judge continued. Thomas heard the compassion in his voice and was grateful for it.

Coleman Philips was one of his father's few friends who had known about the Alzheimer's since the original diagnosis. Unlike some of the others, he hadn't abandoned William after the disease began to progress. The judge still made regular visits, still spent time playing cards or checkers or just reading the newspaper to him, no matter how incoherent and unmanageable William became.

"He's had a rough few days. His nurse didn't think it would be a good idea to drag him out."

Coleman was silent for a few moments, a frown tugging the corners of his wrinkled mouth.

"You and your bride certainly face some tough challenges," he said finally. "But trust me, you'll find them far more bearable now that you have someone to share them with. A good, solid marriage can be an anchor, a safe harbor, in the stormiest of seas. I hope you find that with your young lady, Thomas."

Coleman gave his shoulder a compassionate squeeze. For one strange, surreal moment, it was almost as if the judge were a conduit for William, as if his father was indeed there, lending his blessing to the marriage.

"Thank you," he murmured.

Before the judge could add anything else, Zach tugged on his pantleg. "This is boring and I'm starving. When can we go home and have something for lunch?"

Both men laughed at the exaggerated expression on the little boy's features. "Good question," Tom said. "Should we go find your Aunt Sophie and the girls and see if they're ready to go?"

Zach nodded and slipped his hand in Tom's and he thought again how right those little fingers seemed there.

Ten minutes later, he ushered them into the waiting limousine and they headed back toward Seal Point.

He and Sophie still had not shared more than a few words. If not for the chatter of the children, he thought the ride home would have been completed virtually in silence.

Though he had arranged with the car service for two limousines for the journey to Coleman's office after Mrs. Cope had insisted it was bad luck for him to see his bride before the wedding, he had dismissed one driver so they could all ride together back to Seal Point. Now he and Sophie sat together in the rear-facing seat while the children sat across from them.

Though she said little, he was intensely conscious of her. The curve of her jaw, the lush, exotic scent that always seemed to cling to her, the subtle, tantalizing press of her knee against his whenever the limousine turned a corner.

A few times he sensed her looking at him but before he could catch her at it, she would quickly turn back to the children.

Was she regretting this make-believe marriage, wondering what she'd gotten herself into? He couldn't read anything in the serene cast of her features.

The rest of the day stretched out ahead of them. If this were an ordinary wedding, they would have been preparing to leave on some exotic romantic honeymoon.

Somewhere tropical, maybe, with palm trees and brilliant blue water and deserted white sand beaches where they could walk hand-in-hand in the moonlight, where he could steal a kiss or two or twenty while the waves lapped at their bare feet and the warm sea breeze kissed their skin.

But then, Sophie had been just about everywhere, so no destination he picked would be truly exotic to her.

Just as well. This wasn't an ordinary wedding. He was going to have to do his best to remember that.

He didn't realize he had sighed aloud until she looked over at him. "Already having regrets?" she asked in a low voice so the children wouldn't overhear.

"No. Well, maybe," he admitted. "I was wishing I could take you to some thrilling honeymoon destination, just the two of us."

She inhaled a quick breath, her green eyes wide, a hint of a blush soaking her cheekbones. "Oh," she murmured. Her gaze locked with his for just a moment and he thought he saw blooming awareness there before she quickly looked away.

He settled back into the leather seat, in a much better frame of mind after that brief, charged encounter. At least he knew his bride wasn't immune to him. That had to count for something. If they had physical attraction between them, surely deeper emotions could follow.

He settled back for the remainder of the ride, more heartened than he had been all day.

His good mood dissipated as soon as the limousine

entered the iron gates of Seal Point, when he recognized a dark-blue sedan parked in front of the house.

"Look, Uncle Tommy. Company!" Zach's neck craned as he peered out the window in an effort to identify the vehicle.

By the sudden alarm flaring in her eyes, he knew Sophie also recognized the vehicle as belonging to their friendly neighborhood FBI agents.

Talk about lousy timing.

"Children, why don't you go to your rooms and change out of your fancy clothes, then find Mrs. Cope and see what she's fixed for lunch," she said when the limousine stopped and the driver opened the doors for them. "After we eat, we'll all do something fun together, I promise."

"Like what?" Zach asked, the visitors forgotten.

Tom spoke up. "Since the weather's cleared, we could go horseback riding down at Molera or to the aquarium or we could take a bike ride over to Bird Rock. Whatever you want to do. Talk about it over lunch and we'll see what we can come up with."

Brimming with possibilities, the children rushed into the house without questioning who might have come to call at Seal Point.

"I have a bad feeling about this suddenly," Sophie said after the children had disappeared inside. "They must have news."

"We won't know what until we talk to them. Come on. Let's get this over with."

When he reached out and grabbed her hand, she sent him a startled, flustered look. After a moment, though, she gripped his fingers tightly—gratefully, he thought— and together they walked into the house.

Mrs. Cope greeted them at the door, all but wringing

her hands. "Those FBI agents are here again. They arrived just a few moments after I returned from the wedding. I tried to tell them this wasn't the best time but they said they would wait. They're in the visitor's salon. I'm so sorry I couldn't seem to persuade them to leave."

"It's all right, JoAnn," Sophie said. She inhaled a deep breath, then pasted a polite smile on her face, the same one she'd been wearing most of the morning. Together they walked into the room and found Herrera and Washburn seated on the couch, talking softly.

Herrera looked up at their entrance. Tom watched the FBI agent take in his dress whites, Sophie's demure, flowing dress and their still-interlaced hands.

She raised an eyebrow. "Your housekeeper was right, obviously. This *is* a bad time. If we had known we were interrupting a special occasion, we wouldn't have insisted on talking to you both."

"We were married this morning," he said.

An expression of surprise flitted across her brown eyes but she quickly veiled it. "I'm sorry we bothered you, then. We can speak with you another time."

"No," Sophie said quickly. "Please. If you have news, we want to know about it."

Herrera exchanged a look with her partner. "I don't think you'll find it very pleasant information to deal with on such an important day. We'll come back."

"If it's bad news, it's not going to matter when you deliver it, now is it?" Tom pointed out. "Today or tomorrow, we still won't like it."

"Trust me, Mr. Canfield. This isn't something you're going to want to hear about on your wedding day."

Sudden apprehension nipped at him. He wanted to agree, to tell them to return another time. If it was bad luck to see his bride before the wedding, it surely couldn't bode well to be forced to hear nasty news just after the ceremony.

"Have you had a break in the case?" Sophie asked.

Agent Herrera hesitated. "I really believe it would be best if we returned next week."

"We have spent two weeks with nothing but unanswered questions." Sophie's hand trembled slightly in his. "Please. If you know anything, anything at all, we would like to know."

Herrera gazed at them both for a moment then sighed heavily. "All right. If you're sure you want to hear this then, yes. There's been a break in the case. Forensics came back from the lab and confirmed the blood we found on Leo Harris's car was a DNA match to Walter Marlowe. When we confronted him with it, Harris finally confessed that he did hit the victim."

"And?" Thomas prompted.

After a long pause, the agent went on slowly. "And he claims he was hired to kill Marlowe. That he was only acting on orders."

"Hired? By whom?"

She met his gaze without emotion. "Peter Canfield."

Thomas inhaled sharply. "He implicated my brother? That's ludicrous! What possible reason would Pete have to kill Walter? The man was invaluable to Canfield!"

"Harris didn't know details. He only said that he had done some other work for your brother in the past, most of it unsavory if not downright illegal. Peter contacted him several weeks ago about taking out Mr. Marlowe and he agreed to carry out the hit for twenty thousand dollars. According to him, your brother paid half before the hit but reneged on the other half after the job was done. That's why Leo had been trying to reach him before the accident that killed Mr. and Mrs. Canfield."

Sophie's skin had paled. She looked fragile, lost. She slowly disengaged her fingers from his but he was too wrapped up in his own shock to react.

"So this…this Leo person killed Shelly and Peter because he was angry over money he says Peter owed him?" Sophie asked.

"He denies that part," Herrera said. "It doesn't make sense, anyway. If he's telling the truth about the Marlowe homicide, why kill Peter, the man he claims was footing the bill for the hit? That's no way to collect on an unpaid debt."

He couldn't take this in. It was all too huge, too impossible. "He has to be lying. Peter wouldn't arrange to have Walter killed!"

"We have evidence that he's telling the truth. I'm sorry, Mr. Canfield."

"What kind of evidence?"

"Harris still has most of the down payment. It was paid out in cash, hundred dollar bills with consecutive serial numbers that match those in use at Monterey Bank and Trust on a day when Peter Canfield withdrew ten thousand dollars from one of the Canfield escrow accounts."

"So the numbers match. That doesn't mean anything. Maybe Pete paid him for something completely unrelated!"

Even as he defended his brother, he thought of the tangled mess Pete had left behind at Canfield. The missing money, the inaccurate records. And the fact that someone—Peter?—had deleted evidence proving Leo Harris had been in contact with him.

The agents' scenario made a kind of terrible, hideous sense but he just couldn't seem to get his mind around it all.

"What about Peter and Shelly's crash?" Sophie pressed. "If this Harris person wasn't involved some-how, what caused their car to plummet over the cliff off Highway 1?"

"We don't know exactly," Herrera hedged.

"But we do have a theory," Agent Washburn put in.

Irritation crossed the other agent's features, but she quickly smoothed it away. Still, Thomas had the distinct impression she hadn't wanted the discussion to go in that direction.

"What theory?" Sophie asked.

Herrera's mouth formed a tight line. "Mr. Canfield was driving the vehicle at the time of the crash. Given the details of Mr. Harris's story, we believe there is a…possibility he might have acted with intent when he drove into the ocean."

Thomas was only vaguely aware of Sophie's gasp. This couldn't be real. He rose and paced to the window, his thoughts raging and his insides in knots. The whole thing was surreal, ghastly. A terribly twisted nightmare.

"You're saying you think Peter dug himself into such a deep hole he couldn't get back out, so he chose the easy way. And took his wife along with him."

"It's a theory. That's all."

He glared at Washburn, suddenly angry at his placat-ing tone, at both of them for coming here and springing this on them. On their wedding day, for hell's sake. "I'm not an idiot. Agent Washburn. You wouldn't be here if you didn't have some evidence backing up your theory."

How could they even consider this? Peter couldn't have been capable of these appalling things, could he? Orchestrating Walter's death, then killing himself and Shelly? It didn't make sense, didn't mesh with what he knew of his brother.

Though he loved Pete, he had to admit, he hadn't always liked the adult his brother had become. He had watched him grow increasingly self-absorbed as the years passed. Peter could be thoughtless, even cruel, to Shelly and the children at times and barely tolerated William's deteriorating condition.

Still, despite his brother's flaws, Tom just couldn't reconcile the brainiac kid with the fierce competitive streak who used to follow him around with the man these agents suspected Peter of becoming. Someone who could cold-bloodedly order the hit of Walter—a man who had been like a father to them both—and then plunge to his own death beside the mother of his children.

He didn't want to believe it, wasn't sure he could *ever* believe it, no matter what evidence the FBI managed to produce.

"Are you all right, Ms. Beaumont?" Herrera asked. "Or Mrs. Canfield, I suppose I should say."

He turned and saw that Sophie had sunk into a chair, her skin pale, bloodless. Her eyes looked haunted, and he thought maybe she was going to be sick.

Shame washed through him. He was no better than Pete, so wrapped up in his own shock and disbelief that he hadn't spared a thought for Sophie and how the FBI's suspicions would affect her.

She was his wife and should have been his first priority.

He hurried to her and rested a hand on her shoulder intending to console her but she flinched away from the contact.

Pain shot through him. Of course she wouldn't want comfort from him. He was the brother of the man who may have killed her sister.

"I'm sorry to give you such hard news, especially today," Candace Herrera said in her no-nonsense voice. "We really should have waited a day or two."

"You're just doing your job," Sophie said, her voice wiped clean of any emotion. "We understand that. I appreciate you telling us, even though it's difficult to hear."

"We'll stay in touch when we know more," the agent said.

"Thank you."

Tom ushered them to the door, then returned to face his wife.

Chapter 16

After they left, Sophie tried to grab hold of her scattered thoughts but all she could focus on was the terror her sister must have experienced as that car plunged in a free-fall over the cliff.

Oh, Shelly.

Her stomach churned and the dress that had seemed so loose and flowing and romantic earlier in the day suddenly felt restrictive, strangling the air from her chest.

She was still sitting there trying to center her breathing when Tom returned from showing the FBI agents out. He looked drawn, exhausted, and her heart squeezed with sympathy for him.

He sat heavily in the armchair next to her. "Pete wouldn't have killed Shelly," he said after a moment. "He couldn't have. He adored her, Sophie. You have to know that."

Sophie could think of nothing to say in response, her

mind awash in memories of groping hands on her flesh, hot breath in her ear. She was the last person who could defend anything Peter Canfield might have done. She knew exactly what he was capable of doing.

Tom talked about how much his brother had loved Shelly. She wanted to shout out her denial. What kind of love led a man to act as he had, attacking his wife's sister just a few weeks after the birth of his daughter? That wasn't love or anything like it.

"It was an accident," Thomas went on, although he sounded as if he was trying to convince himself as much as her. "That's all it could be. Pete might have been selfish sometimes—manipulative, even—but he wasn't a murderer."

She made a noncommittal sound and he glanced at her. "I'm so sorry about this. Hell of a wedding day, isn't it?"

To both of their surprise, his ironic tone surprised a laugh out of her. "You could say that."

He studied her for a moment then startled her further by standing up and pulling her into his arms. He was warm and solid, the most dependable thing in her world just now, and she settled against him with a sigh, her arms around his waist.

"We're in this together now, Sophie," he murmured against her hair. "Whatever we eventually find out about the accident, the two of us can deal with it."

How long had it been since she'd been part of an "us"? Since Shelly had married Peter and Sophie had taken off on her own. She hadn't realized how very much she had missed being a piece of a greater whole until just this moment.

She rested against his chest, listening to his heartbeat under the fabric of his Coast Guard uniform and wishing she could find the courage to tell him about that horrible night with Peter, about the reason she had left Seal Point so abruptly.

She couldn't, though. If she told him and he didn't believe her, she thought it would shatter her.

And if he *did* believe her, she knew the revelation would destroy any positive memory he might have left of his brother. Given the direction the investigation was apparently taking, she had a feeling Tom would have very few of those left.

"Are you regretting going through with this—marrying me—now that the FBI believes my brother might have been a murderer?"

She saw uncertainty and doubt in his silvery-blue eyes and wanted to soothe it away.

"No," she said honestly. "Whatever Peter may have done in the past has nothing to do with this, with the future and what's best for the children. On the contrary, if what the FBI says is true, they will need love and support and stability from us more than ever."

When he said nothing, she tilted her head up and found him watching her, an unreadable look in his eyes. Before she could ask him about it, he lowered his head and kissed her.

His mouth was warm and she tasted a memory of the champagne the judge had pressed on them.

His kiss was tender, sweet, and answering emotions welled up inside her, threatening to spill free. She returned the kiss, her arms tight around him. Her husband. She could hardly believe they were married. With sudden fierceness, she wanted this to work, wanted them to be able to build a good, happy life for the children out of the ashes of their tragedy.

Wanted to build that life with him.

Need and desire and love tangled through her and she sighed against his mouth. The sound seemed to spur a change in his kiss, from slow and gentle to hot, intense.

She pulled him closer, and for several long, drugging moments they fused together, lost in each other. Through the heavy sounds of her ragged breathing and her pulse in her ear, she gradually became aware of another sound intruding—giggles.

She wrenched her mouth away, grateful nobody's hands had yet strayed into any embarrassing territory and half turned in his arms toward the doorway.

The children stood watching them, Ali with dreamy stars in her eyes and the twins both covering their mouths with their hands to hold in more of their giggles.

She cleared her throat to draw Tom's attention to their interested audience. He pulled away with a low, heartfelt groan but kept her tucked under one arm.

"Are you guys all done being mushy?" Zach asked.

"For now," Tom answered, his arm still slung over her shoulder.

"'Cause you said we could do something fun today."

"I *was* doing something fun," he muttered, loud enough only for her to hear. She was mortified by the blush she could feel soaking her cheeks and wondered what had happened to the sophisticated, cosmopolitan world traveler she had always considered herself.

"Your uncle and I still need to change and then we'll figure out what to do," Sophie said quickly.

"Can we go out on one of the whale-watching cruises?" Ali asked.

"I want to ride horses and be cowboys," Zach put in.

"Aquarium! Aquarium!" Zoe cried, jumping in place and waving her arms.

"How about we drive up to Santa Cruz to the board-

walk and go on some of the rides?'' Tom suggested, an
idea that immediately met with universal approval.

"Just give us a moment to change," he said to the
children, then dropped his arm from her shoulder and
walked with Sophie out into the hallway.

He kissed her one last time before she headed to her
room, her insides sighing and quivering like she had
already climbed off a twirling amusement park ride.

As wedding days go, this one was certainly unique.

Tom tilted the SUV's rearview mirror and spared a
look from the dark road just long enough to see all three
of the children were cuddled together in the back seat,
sound asleep.

He never would have imagined he would be spending
his wedding night with three sleeping chaperons.

But then, nothing about this particular wedding was
ordinary. He supposed it was only fitting that they had
spent the entire day with the children since they were
the reason for the wedding in the first place.

"It's been a long day for them." Sophie was just a
quiet voice in the dark coming from the seat next to him
and he wondered what was running through her head.

"A long day but a good one, don't you think? For the
most part, anyway."

She was silent for a moment. "Yes," she finally murmured over the muted jazz flowing from the stereo
speakers. "The boardwalk was a great idea. The children
loved it."

"I seem to remember somebody else screaming with
glee on the Giant Dipper."

Her laugh was low, as sultry as the jazz, and vibrated
through every inch of him. "I'm a sucker for roller

coasters. I'm afraid you married a bit of an adrenaline junkie."

"You want adrenaline, you should try to hold a Dolphin steady while you drop a rescue diver in the middle of thirty-foot swells and fifty-knot winds."

He was addicted to her laugh, he discovered. "I believe I'll leave the daring rescues to you," she said.

"This, from the woman who spent two weeks wandering through the Colombian countryside on her own, documenting rescue efforts after that earthquake a few years ago?"

"Good heavens, how did you know about that? I never said a word to Shelly about that trip! She would have been terrified if she'd known."

He wasn't sure how to answer. How much of his emotions would filter through whatever he said? "I might have tried to follow your career a little," he finally admitted.

She was silent, the hum of the children's breathing and the tires spinning through the dark the only sound inside the vehicle. "Why?"

Because I've been crazy about you for a decade.

Of course he couldn't voice the thought, so he offered an answer that was true enough, just not the whole story. "Your photos move me. I can't explain it."

Her eyes were wide, so huge he could see a rim of white around her pupils, but she said nothing.

"And I suppose I thought that maybe if I looked at your work closely enough, I could find my way into your psyche," he went on. "I don't know. Maybe subconsciously I was hoping somehow I could figure out what I did to make you leave ten years ago."

She reached out to touch his arm. "Oh, Tom. You

didn't do anything! The reasons I left had nothing to do with you. Nothing!''

"Then why won't you tell me why you couldn't wait to get away from Seal Point?" Frustration sharpened his voice. "I was falling in love with you, Sophie. I've never said that to another woman. Never had those feelings for another woman. I was falling in love with you and I would have been willing to swear on every Bible in California that you felt the same way.''

"I did," she whispered.

"Then why leave?"

"I can't…" Her voice broke off. "There were …circumstances. Circumstances that had nothing to do with you or my feelings for you. Please, can you let it go at that?''

"I'd like to. But I have to admit, part of me wonders what will happen if those *circumstances,* whatever the hell they were, come up again? Will you leave again? Walk away from me *and* the children this time?''

"No! I told you I wouldn't leave. We're married now, Tom. That means something to me. And besides, the…the circumstances behind why I left won't happen again. They're gone now.''

He wished like hell that he could see more than just the profile of her delicate features in the dim greenish light inside the SUV. He wanted to search her eyes, to push her harder about what she was keeping from him.

If he couldn't learn to trust her, how would they ever make this marriage work?

"It was hard for me, Sophie. After you left, trying to figure out what happened.''

A thick tightness swelled in her throat at the pain in his voice. When she had left, intent only on fleeing Peter's unwanted touches and William's malice, she hadn't really thought Thomas would regret the abrupt end to their brief relationship.

She had wronged him terribly, and she wished more than anything that she could tell him her reasons. Starting out with secrets festering between them wasn't a good beginning for any marriage, especially one on such a shaky foundation as theirs.

"I'm sorry," she whispered.

He was silent, probably waiting for her to add something else to what she knew was a grossly inadequate apology. Before she could think what she could tell him, Ali stirred in the back seat.

"Are we almost home?"

"Just about, pumpkin," Tom said after a brief pause. "Another mile or so."

"Okay." She settled back against the seat and they drove in silence for a few moments then Ali spoke again. "Hey, you guys, thanks for taking us. I had lots of fun at the boardwalk, even if it was kind of a weird thing to do on your wedding day. Taking us all along, I mean."

"We had fun too," Sophie answered. "We're a family now, Al. We do things together. That's what families are all about."

"You know, I was really scared at first. After…after Mom and Dad died. About what would happen to us and everything, I mean. It's good to be a family again."

Tears welled up in Sophie's eyes at the words. "It is, isn't it?" she said with a little sniff she couldn't control.

To her surprise, despite their lingering tension, Tom reached out between them and grabbed her hand in a comforting squeeze. For the remainder of the drive, they stayed that way, with their fingers entwined and unanswered questions just below the surface.

*   *   *

Sophie closed the door to Ali's room softly behind her, certain the girl had drifted to sleep as soon as she had pulled the covers up to her chin. She turned in the darkened hallway toward the twins' room to check Tom's progress getting them into their pajamas.

"Ali get to sleep okay?"

She jumped at the voice coming from the dark.

"Sorry," Tom said. "Didn't mean to startle you."

"I wasn't expecting you to be finished with them already. Usually it takes twenty minutes just to get one of them into pajamas."

"They're both beat. I think that's about the most subdued I've ever seen those two."

"We make a pretty good team, don't we?"

"Yeah. Yeah, we do." He paused. "Would you like a drink or something? Mrs. Cope left some champagne chilling downstairs for us."

Heat soaked her cheeks, though she wasn't exactly sure why. She was glad it was too dim here in the hallway for him to be able to notice. "That was sweet of her."

"The woman has worked here as long as I can remember and I have to admit, I never realized she had such a romantic soul."

An awkward silence descended between them. Technically this was their wedding night. At last they were alone and suddenly she didn't know how to act, what to say. What he expected of her.

"Champagne would be lovely," she said quickly.

He led the way to the kitchen where they found a tray waiting for them with a single white rose in a Waterford vase, two elegant flutes and a magnum of fine champagne.

He popped the cork and poured for her. "What should we toast to?"

She mulled it over for a moment. "How about to new families and second chances?"

His slow smile went a long way to calm her sudden nerves. "Perfect. To new families and second chances."

She returned his smile and had only taken one small sip when he took the glass from her and set it down on the counter behind them, then his mouth replaced the flute against her lips.

He tasted fizzy, heady, and made her as light-headed as if she'd consumed the entire magnum by herself.

"I've been waiting all day to do that again," he murmured against her mouth.

"I've been waiting ten years," she admitted softly.

Something hot and dangerous kindled in his eyes and he kissed her again. She leaned into him, her arms around his neck, and desire exploded between them.

With a groan, he nudged her back against the counter until she was caged by his body. His arms wrapped tightly around her, molding her curves to his hard strength, and his mouth tangled with hers again and again, until she was gasping and trembling with need.

Even that close contact wasn't enough. With effortless ease, he lifted her onto the counter and stepped between her legs. The change in position brought his body into intimate, tantalizing contact with hers and shivery sensations cascaded through her wherever their bodies touched.

His hand reached between their bodies and found the curve of one breast and she murmured his name on a gasp.

He drew back at the sound and growled an oath. "We

can't do this here. Anyone could walk in on us. Mrs. Cope, Maura, one of the kids.''

"We're married," she said somewhat breathlessly. "It's legal."

"Maybe. But I prefer a little privacy, where I'm not likely to be interrupted just as we might be getting to the good parts."

"They're all good parts, aren't they?"

He laughed, a low husky sound that did delicious things to her nerve endings. "With you they are."

She was still smiling as he kissed her again then her smile turned to a laughing gasp as he scooped her into his arms and carried her down the hall to his bedroom.

The room was elegantly comfortable just like all the other rooms at Seal Point, with a four-poster bed and a small sitting area. It was lit only by a small stained-glass lamp burning above the fireplace mantel that sent colored shadows dancing around the room.

She barely registered the furnishings or the play of light, too wrapped up in his kisses.

"We forgot the champagne," she pointed out as he lowered her to the wide bed.

"I don't think we need it, do you?" He slid a hand under the material of her shirt to explore the skin just above her waist.

"Good point." She sucked in a shuddering breath as he deftly worked the buttons of her shirt. She wore only a lacy white cotton bra underneath and he drew it aside.

"You're more beautiful than I remember," he murmured.

"It was dark down on that beach. You couldn't have seen much."

"The moon was bright enough to burn your image into my mind for a decade."

He slid the shirt over her shoulders then cupped her with his powerful hands. She closed her eyes, rocked by the intensity of her need for him. His fingers moved over her skin, tantalizing, teasing, then he lowered his head and tasted her.

With a small cry, she buried her fingers in his hair and held him close while his mouth and lips and tongue drove her crazy with need.

Finally she couldn't endure the torment any longer. Her body ached and trembled and she yearned for closer contact. She tugged at his knit Polo shirt, impatient to feel him, but couldn't manage to pull it over the width of his shoulders.

"Need a hand?" he asked, his breath warm and erotic against her nipple.

"Yes, actually."

"*Semper Paratus*. That's the Coast Guard motto, did you know that?"

"Um, no." She blinked, a little disoriented by the direction of his conversation, especially when each word stirred more nerve endings in her skin and made her nipples tighten and ache.

"It means *always ready*."

"That's a lot of pressure for a guy, isn't it?"

He laughed. "Yeah, but we're up to it. If you need help, call on the Coast Guard."

"Good to know. Thanks." Her voice was thready, breathless. "Could you please help me remove your shirt, Lieutenant?"

He laughed and withdrew far enough to pull his shirt over his head and toss it to the floor. The rest of his clothes quickly followed. She only had a moment to sigh in appreciation of all those firm muscles before he returned and helped her out of her clothes.

Now she was free to touch him, to learn his hollows and angles and textures as he learned hers. She wanted to spend forever right here. Ten years ago she had been young and unsure of herself, afraid to reveal her ignorance. This time she would take all the opportunities she missed that first time with him.

They kissed and touched and explored until both of them were trembling with need. Finally, when she thought she would shudder apart if he didn't come inside her soon, he slid over her and suddenly there he was stretching her, filling her, devastating her.

"Oh, my," she murmured, earning a strangled laugh from him.

"Is that a good *oh, my* or a bad *oh, my?*"

"It's a 'please-don't-stop' *oh, my.*" She gasped as he moved inside her.

"If I have to stop, I'm a dead man." He kissed her again and her hips rose to meet him. They moved that way, bodies and mouths intertwined, while primal need pulsed inside her like the ocean waves two hundred feet below, crashing and pounding at her until she couldn't think, couldn't breathe, could do nothing but drown in his arms.

The waves crested higher and higher and she spiraled with them until he reached between their bodies and touched her. Her cry echoed in the room as she climaxed, holding tight to him. His body strained above her then he followed her, finding his own release.

"Oh, my," she said again, boneless, weightless, as they floated with the tide.

With a soft laugh, he rolled to her side, pulling her against him. She sighed her contentment as she settled against his hard length.

She wanted to treasure this, being here with him

again. To savor every second of it. Her love for him bubbled inside her like the champagne they'd had earlier and nearly spilled out but she held the words back, afraid to utter them.

Not yet. Someday he might be ready to hear them, to accept the love she so wanted to offer, but she knew he wouldn't believe her now.

She drifted to sleep with his arms tight around her and words of love trapped on her tongue.

Chapter 17

Long after Sophie drifted to sleep in his arms, Tom held her and gazed at the multicolored light from the Tiffany lamp on the mantel.

He was too edgy to sleep. So many emotions crowded through him he couldn't sort them out. Love and trepidation and elation and doubt. She tangled him up worse than a rescue line caught on a trawler's mast.

He ought to be relaxed and easy, content to hold her like this. But the future loomed just outside that bedroom door, dark and uncertain. This was where she left last time, after they had shared this same stunning connection in each other's arms.

He couldn't stop thinking about how he had gone to her room that night after the house was still and quiet and found everything gone. Her suitcase, her camera gear. Everything. The only thing left behind to show she even existed beyond his imagination was a subtle scent lingering in the air, womanly and mysterious and all Sophie.

And a note, he remembered. She had left him a note, savage in its brevity: "I had to run. Sorry. Thanks for a great week."

He had sat in that empty room most of the night drawing her scent into his lungs, wondering what he had done to send her running.

He'd tried to reach her for months in New York but she built a solid wall against him, and he eventually realized he could only bang his head against it so many times. The woman wasn't interested. Eventually he gave up and tried to forget her.

He never had. She had somehow seeped into him. Every time he came home to Seal Point and walked down to that sheltered beach he would remember those staggering moments in her arms and all his unanswered questions.

How would he ever forget this? he wondered. When he was twenty-five, he recognized what they had as something amazing and rare. He knew he had feelings for her then but they were nothing compared to the vast sea of tenderness he found himself adrift on now as he held her and watched her sleep.

He couldn't do this. Restless energy flowed through him and he knew he had to get away from her for a while, if only to regain a little much-needed perspective. After carefully untangling their limbs, he slipped from her side and rose from the bed. She stirred a little but quickly slid back under with a tiny smile playing at her lips.

He stared at her rumbled beauty for a long moment and had to rub a fist over his heart at the rage of emotions there. Finally he dragged his gaze away and yanked a pair of swim trunks out of a drawer. In moments he was channeling all his excess energy into fast, even strokes across the cool surface of the pool.

Trying only to burn off his restlessness, he lost count of his laps sometime around twenty-five. Somewhere around fifty, he slowed, his muscles seething and his breathing ragged, then stopped altogether and turned on his back, gazing up at the night sky as he floated.

It was probably close to 2:00 a.m. on his wedding night and he was out here in the cold night air while his bride waited inside, warm and welcoming. What kind of an idiot was he?

A scared one, he finally admitted. He could risk high seas and hurricane winds without even working up a sweat and had once yanked a HH65 Dolphin with an engine malfunction out of a free-fall ten feet before it would have crashed into the churning sea off Kodiak Island.

But he was terrified of letting himself love a woman who had left him once and might again.

Would she, though?

He focused on Orion there in the heavens. There was the question. She said she planned to stay, that the children needed her. And he couldn't deny he had seen the tender emotions in her eyes earlier as he kissed her. She had feelings for him, he knew she did.

Could he somehow find the courage to trust her? To forget about her rejection of him a decade ago?

He would have to, he realized. Unless he could forget the past, they would never be able to build any kind of future. His distrust would always be there between them, a living, prowling thing.

He loved her. Her sense of humor and her gentleness with the children and her amazing skill behind a camera.

Life without her would be as gray and colorless as a photograph left too long out in the sun.

Somehow he had to swallow his wounded pride and accept that she had reasons for leaving him—reasons, she said, that had nothing to do with him. Reasons she couldn't—or wouldn't—tell him.

If he couldn't do a simple thing like that, he didn't deserve to have her stay.

She awoke alone in her husband's bed.

Sophie reached a hand out but the pillow beside her was cool, empty. She rolled onto her back and gazed at the ceiling. Had he been that eager to leave her, then, that he had left her sleeping in his own bed?

Hurt soughed through her like a bitter wind but she tried to ignore it. She couldn't blame him for escaping. She couldn't expect one shattering moment of intimacy to make up for the way she had treated him.

Where had he gone? she wondered. To the study? Or perhaps one of the children or his father had awakened and she'd been sleeping too soundly to hear.

Maybe Zoe had another nightmare and this time Sophie hadn't been there to squirt the bad dream spray. Guilt pinched at her and she hurried from the bed, quickly finding a shirt of Tom's in the closet, a cotton rugby shirt that swamped her, reaching nearly to her knees.

She padded barefoot out into the hallway but saw no lights on underneath William's door so she headed up the stairs. When she reached the top, she saw a figure just emerging from one of the rooms at the end of the hall.

"There you are," she called softly to him. "Did Zoe have another nightmare?"

Oddly, he froze, his back still to her, and she walked closer, so relieved that he'd been seeing to one of the children's needs and not merely escaping her presence that lighthearted happiness bubbled through her. "I'm sorry I didn't wake when you left. I guess that's what happens when you completely wear me out."

The figure stiffened for a moment then straightened and turned toward her, illuminated by the soft glow from the small lamp always left burning in the hallway.

Sophie stared, her stomach dipping like she was back on the Santa Cruz boardwalk. "P-Peter?"

"Hello, Sophie." For a dead man, her brother-in-law spoke with surprising casualness.

The hallway swayed. "You can't be here. It's impossible. I must be the one having a nightmare."

"You mean you're not happy to see me?"

"No. You're dead." *Wake up. Come on, wake up.*

"Afraid not, Soph. I'm not dead and you're not dreaming."

He walked toward her and grabbed her arm with fingers that were definitely flesh and blood. She swayed for a moment, light-headed, as her pulse raged in her ears. For a moment her vision dimmed and she thought she was going to pass out.

She was still trying to concentrate on breathing when he pushed her into the nearest room—the master bedroom she had been using, she realized, teetering on the verge of hysteria.

Inside, he shoved her into a chair and flipped on a lamp. She was too numb to protest. In the pale yellow light, she could see it definitely was her sister's husband. She couldn't mistake those pale blue eyes or smooth features, although his hair looked shaggier than she had ever seen it and he needed a shave.

She looked for cuts, scrapes, broken limbs, but could see none of those. "How can this be?" Her voice was raspy, harsh. "No one in the car could have survived that plunge over the cliff. The police said so. Your body was washed away and never found."

He snorted. "Don't you watch soap operas? If there's no body, you can be sure the son of a bitch is going to turn up in a later episode."

Her mind couldn't seem to function past the shock. Thoughts seemed to whirl through it like blinding snow in a Nepal blizzard.

"How could you survive it? It's impossible! That car plunged six hundred feet into the Pacific."

He didn't answer and suddenly, horribly, she knew. "You weren't in that Mercedes when it went over the cliff, were you?"

"You always were much smarter than your sister, weren't you?"

She stared at the mild amusement on his face. An instant later, she realized the implications. Peter hadn't been in the Mercedes. Shelly had been alone there, buckled into the passenger seat. He must have steered toward the cliff then jumped out just before the car soared over.

"You bastard," she whispered. "You murdered her."

"Ah, Sophie. Such a harsh word, murder."

She couldn't breathe, couldn't think. "What else would you call it?"

He took the armchair across from her. "Expedience. Necessity. I didn't want Shelly to die. I loved my wife, whether you want to believe that or not—it broke my heart knowing she would have to go over that cliff. But I didn't have any choice. I was backed into a corner with no other way out."

Dear heavens. What kind of horror must Shelly have

experienced in those few seconds while the car plunged into the sea? Her sister's last brief moment on earth had been spent knowing the man she loved had betrayed her in the most grievous way imaginable.

She jerked her mind away, knowing she would sink completely into hysteria if she allowed herself to follow that particular train of thought.

"You hired that man to kill Walter Marlowe."

He raised an eyebrow. "If the police have already figured that part out, they must know all of it, then."

Questions surged through her faster than she could process them. "They're convinced you hired Harris for the job but they haven't figured out why you would possibly want him dead."

His handsome features hardened. "I'll tell you why. Marlowe was an interfering old woman. How's that for a motive? He couldn't leave well enough alone. We started making money. A lot of money. Let's just say not all of it from legitimate sources. I kept telling him I knew what I was doing, to just leave things to me, but he wouldn't stop nosing around. Finally he threatened to go to the authorities with his suspicions. I couldn't let him do that, of course. Again, expedience."

He spoke so casually of killing his wife, of hiring someone to kill an old and treasured friend of the family. As casually as a man talking about discarding a suit in a color he no longer liked.

"An effective solution. The only problem was, I got rid of one difficulty but gained another."

"Harris."

He nodded. "Right again. The man wasn't content with the amount we agreed on. He started demanding more and more and I knew it would never end. He had information about me that would destroy me and I knew he wouldn't hesitate to use it. I couldn't let that happen. I knew I had to plan an escape.''

"Why kill Shelly? She adored you!"

"She loved the kids more. I didn't want to do it but I knew she would never agree to leave without them and there was no way in hell I could make it safely out of the country with a wife and three brats. This way was better. Easier. With Shelly's body inside, nobody ever suspected I could have staged the accident, as they might have done if an empty Mercedes ended up in the ocean.''

Hate and fury roiled up inside her and she fought nausea. Her sweet, loving sister had died so this man could fake his own death and leave the country.

"Why go to so much trouble? You could have just disappeared before the police suspected you. You didn't have to kill her.''

"And spend the rest of my life looking over my shoulder? I don't think so. I'm heading to Europe to start over, not to live some fugitive's hole-in-the-wall existence. I would have left days ago but I need to find something first. Something that seems to have disappeared.''

His hard gaze sharpened on hers and she wondered what he had lost. Another thought occurred to her and she pressed a hand to her stomach as the slick nausea rolled again.

"Have you been here at the house all along?"

Lurking, watching, waiting.

"Next door. The Worthingtons have gone on a three-month-long world cruise and left their house empty. Wasn't it convenient that they gave their neighbor and trusted investment banker their security codes in case of a problem? The timing couldn't have been better.''

So close. Just through the trees. Suddenly she remembered William's frequent, eerie insistence that he had talked to his son. The intruder she saw slipping from the house in the middle of the night the week before. Her mysteriously ransacked suitcase.

Peter must have been coming and going between the two houses at will. And she knew nothing of it.

Zoe said she had seen someone in her room. Had Peter dared search the house while they were all here? Had he come in this room while she was sleeping? Watched her?

He rose from the chair, restless suddenly. He wandered the room, his eyes darting around, and she wondered again what he might have lost. What could possibly be so important that he wouldn't leave the country without finding it first?

"I thought I had everything so carefully planned but the whole damn thing turned out to be a screw-up from start to finish. Where is it?"

She blinked at his abrupt mood shift, from casual, confiding, to harsh anger. "Where...where is what?"

He stopped by her chair and wrapped tight fingers around her arm. For the first time she began to realize she could be in danger. She was the only one who knew he was still alive. He had killed two people already. To what lengths would he go to make sure his existence stayed a secret?

"Where did you hide it?" he demanded.

"Peter, I don't even know what you're looking for. How could I have hidden it?"

"You found the stash, didn't you? And decided to take it for yourself. Where is it?" He shook her arm when she just gazed at him helplessly.

After a moment more of silence, a crafty light entered his eyes. "Come on, Sophie. I'll split it with you. Just tell me where you put it."

"I don't know what you're talking about. I swear I don't!"

"That tacky jewelry box you sent your sister. She never let the damn thing out of her sight. It was on the mantel the day of the crash but when I came for it a few days later after things had calmed down a little, it had disappeared."

"The Russian enamel box? What possible use would you have for that? It's virtually worthless."

"Don't act so innocent. We both know you're not." The pressure of his fingers on her arm increased, reminding her horribly of a decade earlier. Groping hands and hot breath and bitter fear.

"It's not the box itself, it's what's inside," Peter went on. "You know where it is, don't you? I can see it in your eyes."

She pictured the box she had unknowingly given to Ali because the angel looked like Shelly. Ali had taken to carrying it around with her in her backpack so she could feel the comfort of her mother's presence at school. It was probably still in her pack in Ali's room.

"I don't know," she insisted, hoping she sounded convincing.

"You're lying. Where is it? I'm not playing games, Sophie."

Suddenly, to her horror, he produced a small silver handgun. At the sight of it, deadly and cold, fear blasted through her.

The children. She couldn't let him kill her. The children had been through too much loss. This would destroy them.

And Tom. How could she die without telling Tom how very much she loved him? Without trying to make things right between them?

Her mind raced as she tried to come up with a way to escape. If she called for help, who would respond? Tom was the only one in this household of women, children and one frail old man who would be able to protect her but she didn't know where in the huge house he might have gone after he left the bed they had shared.

Besides, if she called out, the children would undoubtedly hear her first. Would Peter hurt his own children? He had killed his wife without blinking, apparently, so she could only fear that he would have no qualms about hurting his children.

No. She couldn't call out.

But perhaps she could convince him she would help him, then somehow slip away and call the police.

She had to try, to protect the children.

"I do know where the box is," she finally admitted. She rose from the chair and eased toward the bedroom door.

"I didn't know there was anything inside it besides old letters. I gave it to Ali so she could have something of her mother's. Thoughtless of me, I know, but I really didn't know. It's probably in her room somewhere. If you'll wait here, I'll get it for you."

He followed her, the gun dangling in his hand. "I'm not stupid enough to let you out of my sight. You'll probably run right to my noble and heroic big brother."

"I won't. I swear, I won't."

"Why should I trust you? You probably tell good old Thomas everything. You were always hot for him. You probably couldn't wait to return to Seal Point after all these years and take up where you left off, to climb right back into the sack with him again."

If she wasn't still warm from just leaving Tom's bed, she probably wouldn't have blushed. But she felt the heat soak her cheeks and knew by the dark amusement in Peter's eyes that he had noticed it, too.

"You're screwing him again, aren't you? That's his shirt you're wearing so you must have just left him. What's the matter, wasn't old Tom man enough for you?"

She drew in a ragged breath but said nothing, only faced him belligerently, her chest heaving with each breath as she did her best to stay calm.

The amusement in his eyes changed to something else, something hot and terrifying. Before she realized what was happening and could step away, he grabbed her arm again, the gun in his other hand.

"Now that you've reminded me, I believe the two of us have some unfinished business. I've been thinking for ten years about this sexy body of yours and remembering how that sweet mouth of yours tasted. This is my last chance to see how good my memory is."

She tried to pull away but again he was too strong. And there was that gun to think about. "What about... about the box?" She hated herself for the quiver in her voice but couldn't seem to keep it out.

"I think it can wait a few minutes longer." To her horror, he began tugging her toward the bed.

"No, Peter. I don't want this. Let me go."

He didn't appear to hear her. His mouth landed on hers as he toppled her onto the bed. Just like a decade ago, she fought and struggled but was powerless against his strength.

He reached for her through the cotton and she gave a muffled shriek just as she saw the door swing open over his shoulder. Relief rushed through her. Tom!

But it wasn't. She saw the stooped, rumpled figure in the doorway and wanted to weep. She only needed this to make this whole scene a bitter repeat of that terrible evening a decade ago—for William to come storming in, slinging accusations and cruel words at her, ordering her to leave Seal Point and his sons alone.

Only this time William wasn't the domineering autocrat he'd been back then. He was only a frail, confused old man.

He stood framed in the door in his striped blue pajamas, his mouth slack and his eyes blank with that lost, baffled look.

An empty shell of a man.

What would Peter do if he saw his father here? She wondered with sudden fear for William's safety. She had to get him away.

Somehow she managed to make eye contact with him. Some glimmer of recognition sparked there as it did at odd intervals, and he opened his mouth to speak to her.

Before he could say anything, she gave a quick shake of her head. "Go," she mouthed to William, praying he would understand her for once. "Go. Find Thomas."

To her vast relief, he disappeared from the doorway. She had no time to be grateful for his safety. One of Peter's hands—the one not holding the gun to her temple—slid to her bare legs and began to climb higher.

In a panic now, heedless of the gun, she struggled harder. Somehow through sheer wild luck, she managed to bring an elbow up and slam it into his face. Blood spurted from his nose and fury erupted on his features. He slapped her and her head whipped back.

The gun returned to her temple, cold metal against her skin. "Do that again and you're dead. Since you've told me where to find the box, I don't have any reason but this to keep you around a little longer."

She shivered at the malice in his voice and her vision

dimmed around the edges. As he reached for her again, she couldn't contain one low scream that burst out of her.

An instant later, Peter toppled across her in a boneless heap. The gun dangled from his fingers off the bed then fell to the floor with a thud muffled by the carpet.

For several seconds she didn't know what happened. Why had he stopped? Breathing heavily, she wriggled out from under his dead weight. To her shock, she found William standing by the bed holding one of the heavy bronze sculptures from the hallway, a freeform, eighteen-inch high depiction of a graceful ballerina in mid-plié.

Had he struck his son with it?

He must have. She could think of no other explanation for Peter to be unconscious. Despite the evidence in front of her, she couldn't manage to believe it.

"Are you okay, Sophie?" William asked formally, so much like the man she knew a decade earlier that she could only stare at him, disoriented.

"I…yes. I think so. Thank you so much!"

He frowned and she thought she saw sorrow crease his features. "That's what I should have done ten years ago. I'm sorry, Sophie. I knew Peter was attacking you that day. I didn't want to believe my son could do such a thing but in my heart I knew. I should never have sent you away like that. I was wrong."

"You saved me this time. That's the important thing." She touched his arm and he mustered a smile.

Before he could say anything else, the door crashed open and Tom rushed in wearing swim trunks, dripping wet.

"What's wrong? I thought I heard a scream." He

stood in the doorway, blinking at the scene in front of him. "Dad? Are you okay?"

His gaze jerked beyond her and William to the figure sprawled on the bed behind them. His jaw sagged and the color leached from his face. "Is that...*Peter?*"

In a matter of seconds, she saw myriad emotions cross his features—disbelief, shock, joy, then a wary unease as he began to realize the implications of finding his brother alive.

Her heart ached for him, for the many horrible truths he would have to face about the brother he had loved.

"What happened? What is he doing here? Is he hurt?"

At the sound of Tom's voice, Peter began to stir. He blinked his eyes open for only a moment before William stepped forward and struck him hard again on the back of the head with the sculpture.

"Dad!" Thomas reached out and yanked the piece from his father and threw it to the floor then grabbed both of William's arms. "Sophie, get out of the way. He's dangerous."

"No. Tom, it's okay! Let him go. He won't hurt me. He was trying to protect me."

"From Peter?"

She didn't know how to answer that without revealing everything. While she was still trying to figure out the words, William spoke and she realized the literate, dignified man who had appeared so briefly was disappearing into senility once more.

"Sophie's my friend. She reads to me and we find Hopkin's roses. I couldn't let Peter hurt her. Not again. Not like he did before."

"What do you mean, like he did before. When did Peter hurt Sophie?"

William said nothing, his eyes blank once more.

"Sophie, what is going on here? When did Peter hurt you?"

She looked away, unable to face him with the truth. She wanted to protect him but she knew the time for lies and evasions was over. "When I was at Seal Point before. Ten years ago. But it doesn't matter now."

She turned back to him, longing more than anything to absorb this pain for him. "We have to call the police, Tom. Peter faked his own death and sent Shelly alone over that cliff. He killed her. I'm sorry."

Chapter 18

Hours later after he had dealt with the police and the FBI and the paramedics called to treat a supposedly dead man for a concussion, Tom went looking for Sophie.

She'd disappeared after giving her statement to the FBI agents, a statement she had insisted on giving in private without him.

Though he still couldn't absorb it all, he knew the gist of what she told them. Tom knew his brother admitted to Sophie that he arranged the hit on Walter then decided he needed to flee when the hit man he hired for the job threatened to expose him.

He knew Peter had also told Sophie that in the process of faking his own death, he had killed his wife to make the accident look more authentic. And that his brother had been hiding in a nearby estate since the accident, coming and going from Seal Point as he looked for a box Sophie had given to first her sister then Ali after Shelly's death.

Inside the box, police had found nearly a million dollars in diamonds sewn into the silk lining. His brother's escape fund, money he had siphoned out of Canfield funds and converted to gems so he could live in comfort wherever he ended up, with a new identity and enough money to set him up in style.

Despite the evidence—and what could be more damning than the very fact that Peter was alive and breathing while Tom himself had seen Shelly's battered and broken body at the crash scene?—he still had a hard time believing any of it could be true.

How could his brother have been so brutally cold-blooded, so ruthless and viciously calculating to murder two people while he managed to conceal his true colors from the world? No matter how hard he tried, Tom couldn't understand how he could share a house with someone until he was eighteen and completely miss the evil lurking inside of him.

So many lives destroyed, all because of one man's unimaginable greed. He couldn't even comprehend the magnitude of it.

He supposed he should be grateful his father wouldn't understand what Peter had done. The shock of finding out his son was a thief and a murderer would have killed William.

The children wouldn't be nearly as easy to deal with. He didn't have the first idea what they could say to Ali and the twins about their father. He was only grateful he and Sophie wouldn't have to come up with the words yet—before the police even arrived, Mrs. Cope had ushered the still sleepy, baffled children to her sister's ranchhouse in Carmel Valley.

She would keep them there until later that evening, until he and Sophie could work out how they could possibly break the news to them that their father had killed their mother.

Sophie.

One of those lives most devastated was his wife. Whenever he managed to catch a glimpse of her while dealing with the authorities, he had been struck by how fragile she looked. Lost. Shattered.

Her delicate features had been pale, her eyes huge, bruised, as she tried to cope with the enormity of what Peter had done and he knew she had to be thinking of her sister's last moments.

He wanted to go to her then, pull her against him and block out all this ugliness. But he couldn't, not with a house full of law enforcement officers demanding his attention.

And then she disappeared.

He hadn't seen her for at least an hour. With mounting concern, he searched the entire house with no success. Though he didn't really think she would leave without talking to him, he even went so far as to check the garage but all the vehicles were there in a gleaming row.

In the empty Seal Point kitchen, he leaned against the counter and tried to figure out where she might be. It only took a moment for the answer to hit him.

Dawn was still an hour or so away but the light was already changing, the shadows softening, as he hurried through the Seal Point gardens. At the top of the long flight of steps leading to the beach he looked down and saw a flash of white below.

She shouldn't have come down these steps by herself in the dark, he thought as he hurried down, holding carefully to the railing. Not when they were slippery with morning dew. Just thinking about what could have happened to her made his stomach churn.

When he reached the bottom he found her sitting on the same fallen log where she had accepted his proposal a week earlier.

Their gazes met for only an instant before she looked back at the sea, only a vast dark emptiness in the pale half light of approaching sunrise. Though she said nothing, she slid over to make room for him beside her on the log.

He leaned against it. "It's cold down here. How long have you been sitting there?"

"A while." Her voice was rough, gritty. "I'm sorry. I probably should have told you where I was going but you were busy and I...I needed to get out of there for a while. I just couldn't be inside right now, in that house Shelly had loved."

"Would you rather be alone?"

She sent him a sidelong look. "It's your beach."

He settled onto the log. A hungry, early-bird seagull cried out over the slap of the waves and a cool breeze that smelled of the sea kissed his skin with moisture as he sat beside her, trying to find words of comfort that simply didn't exist.

Though only a handful of hours had passed, it seemed like forever since their bodies had tangled together, since she had slept so peacefully in his arms. Another lifetime ago, before he knew of Peter's vast, desolating betrayal.

So many lives destroyed.

"Will you tell me what happened ten years ago?" he asked as the seagull cried out above them. "What did Dad mean when he said he couldn't let Peter hurt you again?"

She was silent for so long he didn't think she was going to answer him. Finally she raised a knee, wrapping her arms around it and resting her chin there. "I'm sure you've figured it out."

"No, I haven't. Not really."

Her sigh was only a whisper above the murmur of the sea. "That night after we...after we made love, when I left you and returned to the house, your brother met me in the hallway," she finally said, her voice subdued. "He'd been drinking and became a little too friendly. When I told him I wasn't interested he became angry. Demanding."

His insides turned cold as she confirmed what he hadn't wanted to believe, his last illusion about his baby brother shattered like thin, crackly ice. "He raped you?"

"He didn't get that far. Before he could, your father came into the room. He accused me of seducing both his sons and ordered me to leave Seal Point. I didn't want to go before Ali's christening but he threatened to tell you and Shelly about finding us together. Peter and me. That's why I left, Tom. Not because of anything you did."

He wasn't sure his brain could sustain any more jolts. "You should have told me."

Her laugh was low and held no amusement. "Told you what? That your brother tried to rape me and your father called me a white-trash slut and ordered me out of his house, so I decided the whole Canfield family probably would be better off without me?"

He said nothing and she sighed again. "Maybe I should have told you. But I didn't think you would have believed me over your brother and your father."

Ten years ago would he have been able to accept that Pete could be capable of attempted rape? He didn't know.

"I also didn't tell you because I knew that if I did,

Shelly would find out what a bastard her husband really was. A man who could attack his own sister-in-law while his wife nursed their newborn baby upstairs.''

Fury at his brother burned through him again and he closed his eyes and tried to push away images of Sophie fighting off a much stronger Peter.

"I didn't want Shelly to know. She was happy here and I couldn't destroy that for her."

In the pale light he saw a muscle flex in her jaw. "But maybe I should have told her. If I had, she might have left him and then she would still be alive."

She hitched in a sobbing little breath and his heart shattered all over again. He turned and pulled her into his arms. She slid there willingly, her body trembling with cold and reaction, and he rubbed her arms to keep her warm.

After that one sob, she didn't cry again, just pressed her cheek against his shirt and shivered.

"Don't blame yourself for what Peter did," he finally said. "It's not your fault. You can't know what choice Shelly might have made. Even if she had known, she might have stayed with him."

"I know. It just hurts so much."

He said nothing, just tightened his arms around her. They sat that way for a long time, until the sky began to lighten.

Finally she pulled away from him. "So where do we go from here?" she asked, her eyes on the surf licking at the sand.

He drew in a ragged breath. He'd been thinking of little else since the moment he walked into that bedroom and had seen Peter alive and realized the entire world had just shifted.

Though the words gouged his throat like swallowing

thumbtacks, he forced himself to say them. "I think you and the children should leave. Go to New York or wherever and start over away from here."

She stared at him in stunned disbelief, trying to make sense of his words. He wanted them to leave? Of all the things she might have expected him to say, that option would never have occured to her. She wasn't sure her bruised and battered psyche could sustain one more trauma without completely crumbling apart.

"Why?"

It was the only word she could squeeze out of a suddenly raw throat.

"Think about the kids. It was hard enough on them before, dealing with everyone's pity when the whole world thought both their parents died in that crash. How much worse will it be now, once word gets out what really happened?"

"That their father killed their mother?"

He nodded. "I don't want them to bear that stigma."

Those poor children. She wanted to gather them all close right now and hold them tight against her, protect them from the slings and barbs of a world that could be bitterly cruel.

"We can't just walk away and pretend none of this ever happened. That would be far more damaging to them than the pain of learning to deal with it."

"Maybe. But they don't have to cope with it on the Peninsula, where Peter was so prominent. The scandal here will be huge once this hits the media. I hate to think of three innocent children facing that every minute of their lives."

She saw the wisdom of his argument. But the thought

of leaving him cut at her like jagged coral drawn across her chest.

"Maybe you're right," she finally said. "Maybe a new start would be best for all of us. I can take them back to my apartment in New York until we can figure out a permanent solution."

They sat close enough together on the log that she felt the ripple as his muscles tightened. His features hardened into a taut mask and he gazed out at the sea.

"Okay," he said quietly, and she thought she heard a raw sliver of pain in his voice.

"I'll take the children anywhere you think is best. But not without you."

He swiveled to face her, his eyes shocked. "Sophie—"

"This time if I leave Seal Point you're coming with me, Tom. I won't accept anything else. The children love you and need you."

She drew upon her last reserve of strength and courage and reached out to touch the warm, solid curve of his jaw, stubbled with morning shadow. "And *I* love you and need you."

He stared at her and in the pale predawn light she saw shock and uncertainty and then dawning wonder. An instant later he reached for her and kissed her fiercely.

Joy burst inside her like the sun exploding over the Santa Lucia mountains behind them. This was her husband, the man she loved with everything inside of her— her bones, her blood, her heart.

"I love you, Sophie," he said, his voice ragged. "I fell in love with you a decade ago on this same beach. I thought I was over you until you came back. Since you've been here, I've discovered that although it might have been ten years since I tumbled into love with you, in all this time I somehow never managed to climb back out.''

''I love you, Tom,'' she said again. ''I never would have married you if I didn't.''

He laughed. ''Why do you think I asked you? I might have said it was for the children but the truth is, I couldn't bear the thought of living without you.''

She smiled against his mouth. All the stress and horror of the last four hours seemed to fade away here in his arms and she wanted to close her eyes and just bask in his love, turn her face to it like William did to the sun when he was out in his garden.

She knew they had a long, rough journey ahead of them. It wouldn't be easy helping Shelly's children cope with their mother's death and what their father had done. But this was one journey she would not have to make alone and the realization filled her with sweet, healing peace.

Epilogue

"**Y**ou might want to use that outcropping of rocks there to frame the shot. See it, Al?"

"Yeah. I think so. Will you check the focus for me before I shoot?"

Sophie leaned closer to her niece—crouched behind some of her old camera equipment—and peered through the viewfinder. Through the lens she could see Zach and Zoe laughing and chasing each other like little puppies along the pebbled beach off their Oregon home. Warm fall sunlight flashed gold in their hair and their cheeks glowed with joy and life.

The sun was a little too high overhead for the sweet light of dusk, but she wouldn't have changed a thing in the picture. The twins looked happy, glowing with life, exactly as she hoped they would continue to appear forever.

Sophie stepped away from the tripod and gestured for Ali to come forward. "You're perfect, Al. Fire away."

Ali flashed her a grin, then pressed the shutter several times in rapid succession. The girl was a natural behind the camera, Sophie thought. In the past year she had lapped up any tips her aunt could give her with the enthusiasm of a retriever going after birds.

She had taken up her new hobby so fervently that one entire wall in the hallway of their home was devoted to Ali's photographs. There were pictures of the twins sleeping, their noses pink and their mouths ajar. Of Mrs. Cope elbow-deep in bread dough in the kitchen. Of her new friends at school on a field trip, arms slung around each other's shoulders and the sweet joy of youth in their eyes.

There were also a half-dozen photographs of Sophie and Tom together when they thought no one was watching. Kissing on the beach, kissing in the kitchen, kissing on the porch swing.

One of Sophie's favorites of Ali's photos was one she'd taken of her grandfather and Tom leaning against a rock on the Seal Point beach at Christmastime, one of the last photographs of the Canfield patriarch before he died the day before New Year's Eve of a massive stroke.

So many changes had shaped their lives in the past year, she thought, watching the twins throw stones into the soft surf.

Just a few weeks after William died—and only a month after Peter went to prison under a guilty plea agreement for the deaths of Shelly and Walter Marlowe—Tom received new orders from the Coast Guard, this new assignment to Coos Bay.

She missed Seal Point and the Monterey Peninsula and she knew Tom had struggled with the decision to sell his childhood home but she was so fiercely proud of him. After selling the estate and his interest in Canfield Investments, Tom had used most of the proceeds to repay investors his brother had swindled.

They had made a good life here. Tom loved his new assignment, she was taking the occasional magazine freelance job when she could coordinate it with his leave and school holidays so everyone could go along, and the children were thriving away from the stigma of scandal and tragedy attached to them in Monterey.

She was happy. Joyously, deliriously happy, she thought just as the twins flopped onto the blanket next to her.

"When will Uncle Tommy be home?" Zoe asked.

She leaned down to tie the flopping laces on one of Zoe's sneakers. "Probably not until late, after you're in bed."

"I wish he'd hurry," Zach said. "I want to tell him about the father-son camp-out next week. I can't wait to catch a fish and sleep in a tent and not even have to take a bath for two whole days!"

Sophie had to admit, she wanted Tom to hurry, too. For the past ten days he'd been in Texas on a training operation and she thought time had never passed so slowly. Since their marriage, they'd never been apart longer than one night and she missed him with a bone-deep ache.

"You'll see him in the morning at breakfast, I promise."

"Can we have French toast and hash browns?" Zach asked eagerly.

She laughed and tipped his baseball cap down on his forehead. "How about we wait until after we have dinner tonight before we come up with tomorrow's breakfast menu?"

"Okay," he agreed cheerfully. "I'm starving. Let's go eat."

"Sure. Ali, are you finished with that roll of film so we can go inside?"

Ali clicked off one more frame—of Sophie with the twins cuddled on her lap, she realized—then nodded. "That was the end of the roll right there."

They spent a few moments packing the gear away then walked together toward the sprawling house with its huge gleaming windows and weather-aged cedar.

They were almost to the steps leading to the deck that hugged the rear of the house when Sophie heard a car door out front.

"Uncle Tommy!" Zoe shrieked.

"I don't think so, honey. He's not supposed to be back until…"

The children didn't wait to let her finish. Even Ali lowered the photo equipment to the steps then raced around the side of the house after the twins. With a resigned sigh, Sophie followed them to see who had come to visit.

She turned the corner of the house then felt her heart give a joyful little leap. There he was standing by his Jeep in his uniform, looking dark and masculine and gorgeous with the children—their children—swarming around him. Zoe was in one arm, clinging to him like a little monkey with her arms around his neck and her legs clamped around his waist, and he held Ali and Zach close with the other arm.

Sophie couldn't breathe suddenly and had to lean against the rough cedar planking of the house for support as her muscles went weak. Would he still have this effect on her when she was eighty? she wondered. This twirling, pulsing need?

He caught sight of her then and something warm and brilliant kindled in the silver of his eyes. Their gazes held as she walked forward. When she nearly reached him, he set Zoe down.

"Zach," he murmured without taking his gaze from hers, "why don't you and your sisters take in my gear so I can kiss my girl?"

Zach groaned with disgust at the idea of anybody kissing around him but pulled a duffel out of the Jeep while Ali grabbed a garment bag. Zoe trailed after them up the steps and into the house, complaining bitterly about not having anything to carry, until finally they were inside, leaving Sophie and Tom alone.

He smiled and an instant later she was in his arms. How could his kiss still make her heart race and her blood jump like this after a year of marriage?

"I've missed you like crazy," he murmured. "I couldn't sleep the whole time I was gone because you weren't there beside me."

She thought of her own sleepless nights in their big bed, staring through the skylight and aching for him. Though it was probably small of her, she had to admit to experiencing a little satisfaction that he had suffered, too. "That makes two of us. Maybe tonight we'll both finally be able to get a good night's sleep."

Against her mouth, he grinned that slow sexy smile she loved so much. "Or maybe not."

"Okay. Tomorrow night."

He laughed and kissed her again. "I love you so much. I can't even tell you how good it is to be home."

She thought of the hectic pace of her own wandering life before Shelly's death had forced her to stop, to settle in one place for a while. She used to think she was happy wandering from country to country, village to village, with no one to answer to but herself and whatever photo editor had sent her out this time.

Now she knew that she hadn't had the first idea what true joy was until a year ago, when she had set her suitcases down in Monterey and formed this crazy, wonderful, chaotic family with him.

She smiled at this man she loved with everything inside her and settled deeper into his arms. "You don't have to tell me how good it is to be home, Tom. Believe me, I already know."

*   *   *   *   *

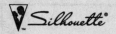

If you enjoyed what you just read,
then we've got an offer you can't resist!

Take 2 bestselling love stories FREE!

Plus get a FREE surprise gift!

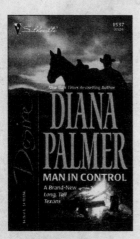

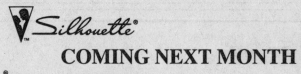

COMING NEXT MONTH

SIMCNM0803